ALL HE NEEDS

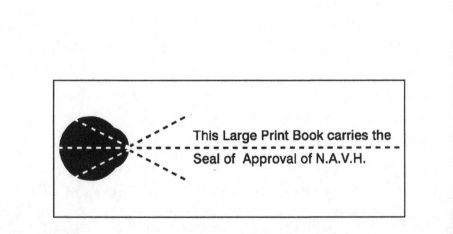

This Large Print Book carries the
Seal of Approval of N.A.V.H.

WEDDINGS BY DIANA

ALL HE NEEDS

SHIRLEY HAILSTOCK

THORNDIKE PRESS
A part of Gale, Cengage Learning

GALE
CENGAGE Learning·

Farmington Hills, Mich • San Francisco • New York • Waterville, Maine
Meriden, Conn • Mason, Ohio • Chicago

GALE
CENGAGE Learning·

LIBRARY OF CONGRESS CATALOGING-IN-PUBLICATION DATA

Names: Hailstock, Shirley, author.
Title: All he needs / by Shirley Hailstock.
Description: Large print edition. | Waterville, Maine : Thorndike Press, 2017. |
    Series: Weddings by Diana | Series: Thorndike Press large print African-American
Identifiers: LCCN 2017007598| ISBN 9781432839529 (hardcover) | ISBN 1432839527
    (hardcover)
Subjects: LCSH: African Americans—Fiction. | African American
    businesspeople—Fiction. | Weddings—Fiction. | GSAFD: Love stories.
Classification: LCC PS3608.A5446 A78 2017 | DDC 813/.54—dc23
LC record available at https://lccn.loc.gov/2017007598

Published in 2017 by arrangement with Harlequin Books, S. A.

Printed in Mexico
1 2 3 4 5 6 7 21 20 19 18 17

Dear Reader,

I love wedding stories. I think I've said that before. In writing the Weddings by Diana series, I've been able to experience a wedding with each book. *All He Needs* is the last book in the series. I hope you enjoy it.

The idea for this story came directly out of the previous Weddings by Diana book, *Someone Like You.* The heroine from *Someone Like You,* Theresa Granville, designed wedding gowns. Creating a place to showcase those gowns was a natural extension. What better place than on the bride?

As you read this story, you'll see how Renee Hart accomplished that feat.

As always, keep reading.

Shirley

To my niece Tanesha
for being there for me.

CHAPTER 1

Renee Hart stepped out of the conference room. She was going to burst. Without a word, she rushed past the secretaries and headed outside. The glass entry doors were the air pressure variety, yet she slammed them both open. Sunlight and humidity hit her like a hot oven. Renee welcomed it as she would a dive into a tropical pool. She needed a place to conceal the echo that was roaring inside her. She walked fast toward her car, but she knew she wasn't going to make it.

She got as far as the tree-lined divider that separated the upper parking lot from the lower one. Then she howled. She let the sound inside her go. All of it. Elation erupted like a volcano. Every emotion she'd ever had thundered and rolled with psychedelic pleasure. She was happy, so happy. Tears broke from her eyes and ran over her cheeks.

Renee hadn't known when she'd accepted the bridal consultant position at Weddings by Diana that it would be the key to her heart's desire.

Two weeks ago she'd presented her idea to the two partners, and after jumping every time one of them opened her door, they'd finally given her the go-ahead today.

Standing under the trees, Renee smiled at the sky through the water in her eyes. The universe had finally favored her. She stood for several minutes, taking it all in. She didn't know how much time passed before she felt the press of heat and humidity on her skin again. Back on solid ground, she returned to the office.

Humming *one more wedding* as if the phrase were the lyrics to a popular song, she pulled up the file for the Griffin–Shephard nuptials on her computer. Twenty minutes later she was still staring at the screen with no idea what she should do next. Yet her mind was racing with things that needed to be done for her new venture.

A bridal magazine. Her own creation. Directed by her. With her ideas. There was so much to be done. Vendors, suppliers, layouts. Did she still have her contacts in the industry? She had to find a place to work, hire people . . . she needed to talk to

Teddy about using her designs in the first issue. *The first issue.* She nearly screamed.

And a name.

What was she going to call the magazine? She had control, complete control — the partners had given it to her. Releasing a breath, Renee threaded her fingers through her hair, holding her long mane away from her face as her thoughts whirled. A boulder-weight of decisions crushed her shoulders. Where was she going to start?

And how long would it be before Carter found out?

Two weeks later, Renee's blood still sang with joy at the prospect of her new job. She was in New York, and she'd had several appointments to get the magazine's plan started. Initially, she'd been overwhelmed, but a little wine and a pen and paper calmed her down enough to begin cataloging the list of things she needed to accomplish. But before everything could begin rolling, she would have to be a consultant on one more wedding she'd already agreed to do. Then she could give her full attention to *Designed for Brides,* the name she'd chosen for the magazine.

The sun had set and she should be out with friends, painting the town as many shades of red as were in the rainbow. But she wasn't. She was walking toward Rockefeller Center, marveling at the heartbeat of the city and remembering the times she'd rushed past all the wide-eyed tourists and crowded commotion without a second thought.

Reaching Radio City, Renee turned toward Fifth Avenue. A couple holding hands raised them in an arch and she ducked through it. Renee looked after the lovers, remembering when that was her. She should have known better than to come to the city. It was too close to Carter. But New York was huge. Nightlife was abundant. There had to be a million places to go on any given night. The chances of her running into Carter Hampshire were minuscule. She was safe. And maybe he wasn't even in the city anymore. He'd told her he was leaving when he'd said he no longer wanted to see her. Maybe he was still away. Gone to parts unknown.

Renee had departed, too. She'd pulled up stakes and moved to Princeton, NJ, where, to her good fortune, she'd joined Diana Greer and Teddy Granville at Weddings by Diana.

But today she was back in the city she considered home. Out of the blue, her friend, Blair Massey, had called and invited her for dinner. How Blair had known Renee was in the city was a mystery she'd have to uncover later.

Renee had a wedding in Brooklyn tomorrow night. She was here to make sure all the final details were in order, but she couldn't help feeling nervous about reconnecting with people from her old life. That was how she thought of it — her old life. Back before she'd gone to Princeton, when she'd spent much of her time with people like Blair and Carter.

Her cell phone played the wedding march. She jerked around toward a shop window and stopped. Just being in New York put her on edge. She relaxed and put the device to her ear.

"Blair, I'm on my way," she said.

"Glad I caught you. I want to change where we meet," Blair said.

"Well, I'm good and hungry."

"I just discovered Villa Maria's is closed for renovations. Let's meet at Moonraker's on 48th Street."

"Fine," Renee said. "I can be there in fifteen minutes."

"See you then."

She felt a little better after hearing Blair's voice. The night had promise. Renee

13

wouldn't think about Carter at all — he was out of her life. He'd been out of it for three years. There was no reason to think that on a Friday night, in a city this size, she'd run into the one man she never wanted to see again. He was probably in the Hamptons or out having fun with someone else.

Still, she couldn't help thinking about him. They'd worked together, then begun dating. She'd been well on her way to falling in love when — when he'd left her. It had been a clean break, nothing drawn out or lingering. No arguments, accusations or tears, yet three years later Renee felt as bereft as she had the day he'd walked out of her life.

She'd cycled through many possible reasons for their breakup: he wanted to marry someone else, his family disapproved of her, there was another woman, maybe he'd discovered he had a child. The truth was, she just didn't know. And without that closure, her wounded heart had no chance of healing.

Carter Hampshire sat forward in his chair and snapped the trade magazine as if he could shake the words off the page. Dropping it on the desk, he steepled his fingers as he looked down over the story. It was a small notice, but the name jumped off the page. He hadn't heard about her in three years. Carter looked down again. Of all the print on that page, his eyes went straight to her name.

Renee Hart, former director of the wedding magazine division at Hampshire Publications, is planning to start her own magazine for brides. The title for the new venture has not been determined at this writing, but Ms. Hart is actively making the rounds.

"Damn," Carter cursed. It couldn't be true. But in his heart, he knew it was something she was fully capable of doing. It wasn't inevitable, but it was logical for Renee. If she hadn't gone to work for one of his competitors, she'd be striking out on her own.

Carter walked to the windows on the 38th floor of the building that bore his family name. The night lights of New York emulated the postcards tourists bought every year.

"Renee Hart." He spoke her name aloud, checking the feel of it on his lips, the sound of it in the empty air. After three years, she still haunted him. A benevolent ghost, whose face and figure was as corporeal as smoke. But in his mind she was almost touchable.

And now she was returning to New York. It made sense that she would return to the city — New York was a publishing powerhouse.

Carter returned to his desk and picked up the office phone. He dialed a number and waited. Blair Massey answered on the first ring.

"Good, you're still there," he said without saying hello. It was seven o'clock, but Blair often worked late. He and Blair had known each other for years. She was a wizard at what she did, and she had mentored Renee. If anyone knew the whole story, it would be Blair.

"I was just on my way out."

"Meet me in the lobby." It was a suggestion, and Carter tried to keep the command tone out of his voice. He hung up.

Blair was waiting when he stepped out of the small paneled room. The fifty-year-old woman looked serious, although she was as impeccably dressed as any model on the fashion pages.

"Carter, I was trying to tell you I already have dinner plans," Blair said. She checked her watch. "And I'm already late."

He took her arm and moved her out of the parade of people. "Where are you eating?"

"At Moonraker's."

"Good, I'll walk with you."

He rushed her along, heading for the door and 48th Street. Blair stopped abruptly and moved to the side. "What's going on?"

"Renee Hart," he answered.

Blair's expression didn't alter more than a millimeter, but the slow breath she exhaled told him she knew.

"What about Renee?" Blair hedged.

"Is she going into competition with us?"

"Where'd you hear that?"

"It doesn't matter. Answer the question."

"She's starting a magazine. It's small stuff. We have no need for alarm."

"I'm not alarmed."

"Then why did you rush down from the 38th floor?"

"The news came as a surprise. How long have you known?"

"A couple of weeks," she said.

"Why didn't you tell me?"

She searched his face a long time. Carter held his expression still.

"It didn't seem that important. When the Weaver Group opened a magazine that competed with our how-to series on home improvement, you didn't consider it news-worthy. Why is Renee's small entry into the bridal market cause for concern? She hasn't even chosen the name of the publication yet. Unless your interest has nothing to do with the business . . ."

Blair was aware of Carter's past relation-ship with Renee. He'd never spoken a word to her about it, but Renee was her friend, and women talked.

She checked her watch. "I'm going to be late. Carter, if you're really interested, I'll find out what I can and call you after din-ner."

"Find out?" he said. "Is Renee here? Are you having dinner with *her*?"

Blair looked at the sky, exasperated that she'd let him guess who she was meeting.

"I'm going," he said and took her arm. Carter should have thought better of it, but when had he ever been rational where Renee was concerned?

"Carter," Blair said. "She may not want to see you."

Carter stopped and thought about that a moment. "More than likely, she doesn't."

Renee loved to walk in Manhattan. The theater crowds were assembling for the eight o'clock performances. While the sun wouldn't set for another two hours, the streets looked like a parade was about to begin. Cabs blew horns, creating their own music, and Renee smiled as she took in the familiarity. She loved New York. She'd missed it. While Princeton had the university and its own personality, New York was incomparable.

Reaching the restaurant, Renee pulled the door open. She stopped the moment she stepped through it. Blair wasn't alone.

She was sitting with *Carter.*

Renee's throat went dry. Even with his back to her, Renee knew it was him. She wanted to turn and run. Every fiber in her body screamed at her to go, back out and walk away. No, *run* away. But her feet refused to follow instructions.

Then it was too late. Carter glanced into the mirrored surface in front of him and made eye contact. Spasms of memories raced into her. Time that had stood still for three years was unleashed. Memories of their entwined bodies on rumpled sheets broke, freely expanding into a new and confusing world.

Renee mentally shook herself. Carter was her past, her old life — not her present, and certainly not her future. She smiled widely and waved, and Carter turned around. The restaurant was dimly lit. She couldn't see the defined features of his expression, but she was sure he'd known she was coming. Blair must have told him, invited him to attend dinner with them.

Her feet suddenly got the message and she moved toward the table. Seeing Carter again had to happen sometime. She would have liked to have been more prepared for it, but tonight was as good a night as any.

He stood as she approached the table. Blair came around and hugged her.

"Carter, this is an unexpected surprise," Renee said. She put her hand out for him to shake, warding off any chance that he might try to hug or kiss her. She didn't want even the simplest embrace from him.

"How are you, Renee?" he asked.

His voice could be her undoing. It was as deep as she remembered it — in the dark of night, after they'd made love, she loved listening to him talk. She thought of the way the sound surrounded her, caressed her like a physical being that could capture and hold her. Renee felt the heat rise in her face and the burn of her ears. She forced the thoughts back.

"Let's sit down," Blair said.

Blair returned to the banquette seat. Renee took a step to follow her, but Carter pulled out the chair next to him. She looked at it for a second before sitting down. This close to him, she could feel the warmth of his hands near her shoulders.

"Blair tells me you've been working in New Jersey," Carter began as soon as the waiter took her drink order.

She glanced at Blair, a silent admonishment in her eyes. "Weddings by Diana," she told him. "It's a consulting firm. I thought I'd see what the other side of the table looked like."

"But now you're crossing back over," Blair spilled.

Renee wanted to throttle her. She quickly glanced at Carter. He was staring at her and didn't appear to have heard Blair's comment. Carter was a key partner in his family's magazine company, and Hampshire Publications had a division dedicated to the bridal industry. Renee had worked there. Along with bridal magazines, there were divisions covering every other aspects of publication. To Carter, her small entry into the market with Weddings by Diana must seem like a teardrop in the ocean.

"What do you do there?"

"I'm a wedding consultant, and now I'm working on a special project." She wanted to be as vague as possible. "How's Hamp-

21

shire doing? Are you back there?"

He nodded. "I've been back a few months."

"I see," she said. But she didn't see. She hadn't seen it when he'd left, and she didn't understand it now. What was he doing here? Why had Blair brought him? He couldn't want to see her again, not after what he'd told her when he'd left. "How's the staff?" She needed something to say to get her mind off their relationship.

"There's been a lot of turnover," Blair answered. "At one point, I had to go back and fill in."

"But things have stabilized now," Carter added.

"Of course, if you want to return . . ." Blair sat forward and looked her straight in the eye. "I'm sure I could find a place for you."

The waiter arrived with their drinks, preventing her from replying.

"Are you open to that?" Carter asked when it was just the three of them.

"Open to what?" she hedged.

"Returning to Hampshire Publications."

Renee wondered if that was the real reason he was at this dinner. Had he come with Blair to ask her to return? And why? The two of them would not be picking up things where they had left off three years earlier. And after the way they'd parted, how could he expect that she would be open to working for him again?

"I'm satisfied where I am for the moment," she said. It was good practice to leave the door open to possibilities, so she did. But she had no intention of ever walking through that door, or even of ever seeing him again.

Their dinner arrived and Renee remembered little of the conversation after that. She was concentrating on the mechanics of eating. Cutting the steak, lifting it to her mouth, chewing and swallowing. Carter's presence unnerved her. Blair should have prepared her for his appearance. The conversation turned to their lives together, the life before. Carter spoke of the long nights in the office closing the magazine, the minor crises they'd averted just in time, the cold pizza they'd consumed when issues took three times as long to finish as expected.

Renee's mind tried to wander to other places — memories of putting the magazine to bed right before she and Carter went to bed — but she blocked those as much as she could. She smiled, laughed at the appropriate places and made a comment now and then to let them know she was listening.

By the time the waiter took dessert orders, Renee noticed she'd only pushed the food around on her plate. She refused dessert but accepted the coffee.

"Renee, how do you find working as a bridal consultant?" Blair turned the subject to the present.

Taking a sip of her coffee, she took a moment to answer. "The brides are a delight," she said honestly. "Their wedding day is the most important thing in their lives, and it was a joy making it happen."

"You didn't find the whole thing a little stressful?" Carter asked.

"No more than the stress of getting a monthly magazine out. For a wedding, I have an entire year to get all the details in place."

What was he trying to do? Renee wondered. Why was he deliberately baiting her? She wasn't the one who ran out on their relationship.

"What about yourself?" Blair commented. "Did working with all those real-life brides make you want to be one?"

Thankfully, Renee was not holding her cup. It was the last question she expected. She felt more than saw Carter turn to listen to her answer. Color flooded her face and burned up her neck to her ears.

"No," she said. It was a lie and she hoped neither Blair nor Carter could tell. "There are too many details that need attention for me to think of anything except the bride's plan. I never even thought of what I might want. Usually I'm just suggesting something to the bride or her mother."

"You must be the exception to the rule," Blair stated.

"What rule?"

"The one that says every woman plans her wedding the moment she enters puberty. I remember choosing my wedding gown while I was still in high school." She smiled as if the happy memory was only a day past. Blair had been married for seventeen years. Renee knew that Blair wanted that euphoric wedding feeling to last forever. That's why she'd gone to Hampshire Publications and had been there so long. When Renee had applied for the job in the bridal department, right out of college, it was Blair who'd given her the opportunity to prove herself. And it was Blair's enthusiasm that had rubbed off on Renee.

"One of the partners, Theresa Granville, designs gowns," Renee said.

"I've heard of her," Blair said. "She's making quite a name for herself."

Renee nodded. "She's had a couple of designs that stopped me in my tracks."

"So, you're interested in getting married." Carter stated it as if it was fact.

"A lot of people are." She skirted the question. "If they weren't, we'd all be out of a job."

He nodded, using that up-and-down movement of his head that was so slight that she wouldn't have seen it if she wasn't already familiar with it. It was Carter's way of conceding the point.

The waiter returned with a pot of coffee. She refused a refill. It was time to put some distance between herself and Carter Hampshire.

"I'm afraid I'd going to have to eat and run," she began. "I have a wedding in the morning so I have to be up early checking the final details," Renee lied. Her wedding was actually in the evening, but she wanted some time to go over every detail. It was her last consulting job and she wanted it to turn out perfect.

Renee stood. Carter stood, too.

"Blair, thank you for dinner. We'll have to do this again sometime." She gave Blair a look that said, *alone.*

"Thank Carter. He's paying."

Renee looked at Carter, but said nothing.

"I'll see you to your hotel," Carter said.

"That won't be necessary. It's not far and Blair needs the escort much more than I do."

Blair stood up. "I have an escort," she said. At that moment, Campbell Massey came through the door as if on cue. Blair went into his arms and they kissed. Then he turned to Renee.

"Renee, it's great to see you." He swept her into his arms for a bear hug. He kissed her on the cheek and set her back with a happy smile. Renee liked Camp. She'd liked him from the moment they'd met almost ten years ago. "You are just as beautiful as ever."

"And you are just as much a flatterer as you've ever been."

"No flattery," he said. "Isn't she beautiful, Carter?"

Both Blair and Camp looked to Carter for an answer. Renee turned from Camp, her body suddenly going cold.

"She's quite ravishing," he stated, his voice low.

To her ears it sounded hungry, sexually hungry. Her knees threatened to turn to water.

"Well, we'd better be off," Blair said, tak-

27

ing Camp's arm. "Carter, you will see Renee back to her hotel?"

He nodded. The couple headed for the door, Carter and Renee trailed them. Out on the street, Renee turned to him. "I know you have a long way to go. You don't have to go with me. I'm not that far from here."

Carter looked over her head. "The Westley?" he said. It was an independent hotel. Renee liked patronizing small businesses. However, she hadn't realized she was so transparent to Carter.

Especially after three years.

But the truth was, he was wrong. She wasn't at the Westley, but there was no need to correct him.

Carter put his hand on her lower back to guide her toward the hotel. She stepped aside, forcing him to drop it. She walked quickly toward the hotel. It was merely three blocks from the restaurant. They covered the distance in silence. Outside the entrance Renee turned to Carter.

"Thank you. It was nice seeing you again." The words were false, but Renee wanted to get away from him as quickly as she could. She turned. Carter caught her arm and pulled her around.

"I want to talk to you."

"I have an early call. I really need to go,"

she said.

"I remember when we spent long nights together and still made deadline."

Her head whipped up and she stared at him. "We were different people then," Renee said. She was in love then. He was not.

Carter pushed open the door to the hotel. He was right behind Renee. She had to move or feel his body form-fitted to hers. Avoiding the bar, she went to a collection of chairs near the back wall.

"What is it you want to talk about?" Renee asked.

He sat, leaned forward and rubbed his hands together as if it was cold. Then he looked her straight in the eye. "Are you sure you want to continue with weddings? You could just as easily return to Hampshire."

It wouldn't be easy and she knew it, even if he didn't. Renee took a moment, probing Carter's face for something to give her a clue to his motives. She found nothing. But she felt there was a meaning under his words. She couldn't pull it into focus, but Carter wanted something from her. She just didn't know what it was — yet.

"Renee?" he prompted.

"I've already given you my answer."

"But have you thought about what I'm offering?"

"No, Carter. Why don't you tell me? Just what is it you're offering that you think will entice me back to Hampshire Publications?"

Carter adjusted his position, clasping his hands between his knees. Renee's instinct was to move back, allowing herself more personal space. At the last moment, she decided to go on the offensive. She moved in closer as if they were conspirators about to exchange the plans for a secret weapon.

"First, you're in charge of everything." He spread his hands. "The entire bridal division is yours."

"And I would report directly to you? That is, I assume you're the head of editorial."

He nodded. Renee thought she saw the faintest look of smugness on his face.

"We've worked together before and that proved beneficial."

"That's not a positive," she told him and was rewarded by seeing his face fall. It was only for a moment, and only someone who knew his features intimately would have noticed it.

"Whatever you're being paid by that little business, I'll double."

Renee stood up. Carter got to his feet, too. She didn't like the way he'd insulted her business, as if only a huge company like his was worthwhile. Pointing out that his father had begun the huge empire would have been a waste of breath.

"Money," she said. "You think you can find my price, and I'll just return to Hampshire Publications." She shook her head, a satisfied smile edging the corners of her lips up. "I'm not for sale, Carter. And especially not to a Hampshire."

CHAPTER 2

Her last wedding. Renee watched as the
new Mr. and Mrs. took their places on the
dais as the reception began. Everything
about the wedding had been technically correct.

Renee had had no complaints, hadn't had
to talk anyone down from a frantic rethink-
ing of what marriage meant. She'd had no
supplies arrive late, no mishaps with the
bride's gown, no groom needing to be
reminded of when and where to stand and
no issues with any of the bridesmaids. The
mothers of both the bride and groom com-
plimented Renee's efficiency. Everything
was going like clockwork. For a wedding
consultant, it was nirvana — the type of
execution they lived for. Perfect. The bride
beamed and the groom's smile
was from ear to ear. It was exactly the
swan song she wished for.

But all that efficiency did was leave her

time to think about Carter. She'd tried for the last three years to put him out of her mind. She'd thought she'd done it. That was, until she'd seen him sitting at the dinner table last night. Her heart had thudded against her ribs so hard she'd thought he would be able to hear it.

It was frightening that he knew where she would choose to stay. The only reason she wasn't at the Westley was because Weddings by Diana had an unoccupied guesthouse available. They used it for brides who were from out of town and needed a place to dress before the ceremony. Occasionally, brides came into New York to check out accommodations. The guesthouse was part of some of the high-end packages.

Renee had allowed Carter to believe she was at the Westley. She'd even gotten on the elevator, but only ridden it to the mezzanine. After ten minutes she'd slipped out the back entrance and taken a taxi to the guesthouse.

A burst of laughter brought Renee back to the festivities. The bride and groom were laughing, yet the love in their eyes as they looked at each other was visible. Renee felt her own eyes mist over. For a moment, she saw herself as the bride and Carter as her groom. She blinked, shaking the image free.

33

It was time to go.

Her last act was to let the bridal party know she was leaving and to make sure there was nothing left undone. Renee's smile was wide as she congratulated the couple, said her goodbyes and started the walk back to the car that would return her to the Brides by Diana guesthouse.

She hadn't thought she'd be as emotional as she'd been throughout the day. Maybe it was because she knew it was her last wedding. She'd even repeated the vows to herself as the minister spoke them. Or maybe it was her mixed feelings about the changes ahead. Although she was excited about the magazine, there was also a certain amount of fear in her mind.

She also thought of Carter and Blair, and their question about her feelings on weddings drifted into her mind. As she'd listened to the couple's vows, they seemed to have more weight than in the past. Did it have anything to do with Carter suddenly reappearing in her life?

There was a time when she'd entertained the thought of marriage. She'd fantasized about it, but that's as far as it had gotten. Even after moving to Princeton, seeing all the brides in their gowns made her imagine walking down the aisle with Carter.

It was safe, she told herself — she was leaving New York in a couple of days, regardless of what she'd said to Carter. She'd be back occasionally, and it was inevitable that they would meet at the same events. But Renee would be able to see him across a room and not have her heart jump.

Carter had changed. Gone was that boyish quality that used to vie for dominance on his face. His expression was more serious than before. His hair was shorter and the mustache that used to tickle her nose had been replaced with a clean-shaven look. He'd been on the basketball team in high school and college, and his body today still had the lean hardness of a twenty-year-old.

Renee wondered where he'd been for the last few years. He'd blown her off as if she were nothing to him. So why was it she still felt as if there was some unfinished business that needed closure? Carter had told her there was nothing between them. And there wasn't. They'd never gotten to the point where things change for better or worse. The place where you decide if you want to step over a line, or you realize the relationship has no place to go.

He hadn't waited for that moment. Carter knew earlier than the launch. And he'd spared her from any further involvement. At least, that's what she'd told herself. So what now? Why was her mind stuck on him and when she'd see him again? She thought their discussion last night would have discouraged him from trying to convince her to return to work at Hampshire.

Yet he'd called her cell phone during the ceremony and insisted on meeting with her at her hotel. No doubt he'd gotten the number from Blair. If she'd had time to banter with him, Renee would have refused the meeting. But in the back of her mind she knew she wanted to see him.

Back at the guesthouse, Renee changed from the suit she'd worn to the wedding. She wanted Carter to see her in control, happy with herself and commanding her own future. She put on a straight red dress and added a pearl necklace and matching teardrop earrings. She swung her hair up and to the side, anchoring it with a wavy pearl comb. Checking her image in the mirror, she left the town house in time to meet him in the hotel lobby.

Carter arrived through the revolving door just as she stepped off the elevator and waited. It was all she could do to keep her breath from leaving her body. The contrast of his dark suit and white shirt emphasized his skin. She took in the broadness of the shoulders she used to lay her head on. If he'd gained an ounce in three years, she'd need a microscope to find it. He started toward her. Renee remembered his easy gait, the confidence that wrapped around him like a second skin.

What hadn't changed was his smile. White teeth gleamed at her, and try as she might, she had to return it. He stopped two feet away. Despite her five-foot-five-inch frame and the heels that raised her up four additional inches, she still had to look up at him to see his face.

"You look beautiful," he murmured. It was a whisper, so low she barely heard it.

Renee felt the rush of heat flush her cheeks.

"Thanks. You're quite the figure, too."

He moved a step closer to her. Renee instinctively knew he planned to embrace her. The thought made her both excited and scared.

Taking a step back, she said, "Don't."

Carter stopped. "I was only going to kiss your cheek. Isn't that what friends do? And we've known each other for years."

"No, we haven't." She shook her head. "We're strangers."

"Strangers?" Carter's brows rose.

"You've been gone for three years. For all

I know, you could be married with three children. The same could be true of me. So we are strangers. You've changed. I've changed. We're not the same people we were three years ago. You wouldn't hug someone you'd just met. So consider me that someone."

Carter took a step back. For a long moment he stared at her as if assessing who this new woman was. Renee withstood his scrutiny.

"I thought we'd go to Mile's End."

"My last wedding was today, and I'm leaving early. Would you mind eating here?" She gestured toward the restaurants that were at the back of the building on the ground floor. "I've already made us a reservation."

Carter shrugged and smiled. Renee understood that she'd thwarted his plans. She had plans of her own, and traveling to a place they'd spent time together wasn't on her agenda.

"I must admit, I was a little surprised to find you on the other end of the phone asking me to meet you for dinner," Renee said when they were seated.

He smiled. It didn't reach his eyes.

"I'm glad you came."

"Why is that? What do you want to talk about? I was sure we'd settled everything last night."

He took a moment to gather his thoughts. Renee wondered if this meeting had something to do with them as a couple. There was no *them*. There had never really been a *them*. She'd thought there was, that there could be, but obviously Carter had other plans.

"Your name has come up several times in the last few days," Carter said.

She didn't react. She waited for him to go on. "Come up where?"

"Along the avenues of publisher's row. There's a rumor going around that you're going into competition with me."

Renee leaned forward. "With *you*?"

"With my company."

"What kind of competition? There are several different kinds of businesses you're responsible for."

"Magazines," he said. "Specifically bridal magazines."

Renee smiled. She picked up her glass of wine and took a sip. Then she replaced it and sat back. "Not a rumor," she said.

"It's not a rumor?"

"Can't be a rumor if it's true." She waited a moment, then asked, "Weren't you listening last night when Blair mentioned my new job?"

His brows rose in surprise. "I didn't think she was serious."

Renee stared at him. "And the notice in the trades?"

She knew Carter read all the trade publications that detailed news about the various magazines Hampshire sold. He had a huge capacity for remembering and recalling what he read, and Renee knew he wouldn't miss the small paragraph bearing her name.

"You are serious?" he asked rhetorically.

"Don't look so surprised. I'm fully capable of running a magazine. You should know that. I ran Hampshire's division for three years."

"You're very capable."

"So, why are we here?" She spread her hands.

Again Carter waited a long moment before speaking. Renee wondered when he'd picked up that habit. He was usually decisive, in control, always knew what to say, how to act.

"I want you to come back to Hampshire Publications."

"You have got to be kidding," Renee said, her voice breathy and low. "We've already talked about this. I'm perfectly happy where I am. Why would I come back to Hampshire?"

"It's a profitable company, and it's a place where you fit in. You know some of the employees and they all respect you."

Renee looked at him. She knew Blair Massey. But with three years gone, she might not know most of the people anymore. Magazine publishing was a place that lent itself to turnover.

"Is Hampshire in trouble?" He'd said it was profitable, but that didn't mean the bridal division was afloat.

Carter shook his head. Renee looked for any sign of slowness, any inkling that he was hiding something. She found nothing to make her believe he wasn't telling her the whole truth.

"You're great at seeing what works and what doesn't in the magazine. Your ideas are always good and sales took an upward climb when you put your mark on the magazine. You could have the whole package with us. I can't imagine you would want to compete with us."

Hackles went up on the back of her neck. "I'm just a little business," Renee began. "In fact, at this point, I'm still scouting out the business. You're a conglomerate with magazines, textbooks, novels, comics and a score of peripherals. You can't be afraid of me."

41

"It's not fear. Hampshire wants you to be comfortable, and we don't want your reputation to suffer with a start-up."

"Well, that takes the cake. You believe that nothing outside of your control is worthy of doing?"

"I didn't say that."

"Didn't you?" She stopped and narrowed her eyes. "You said Hampshire wasn't in trouble. What about the bridal division? Has there been a dip in sales?"

Again Carter sat forward and looked at her. "I'll be frank with you. The division could do better. When you were directing it, it was at the top of the market. We've lost some market share — not enough to be concerned about. But we don't want to lose any more. Bringing you onboard would ensure that."

"Thanks for the vote of confidence, but —"

"Don't answer yet." He stopped her with one hand up. "Think about it overnight. Give yourself time to get used to the idea. We can meet tomorrow."

"I won't be here tomorrow," she lied.

"Renee, can't you give me a few minutes, lunch or dinner? Princeton can't have that great a need for you that you can't spare an old friend a few hours."

Renee felt guilty, although she had no reason to. She wasn't actually leaving until Sunday, and other than additional planning, she had a morning appointment tomorrow. After that, there was no one she could call, no arrangements she could make until Monday. But she didn't want Carter to think his presence influenced her in any way.

"All right, Carter," she said. "I'll meet you tomorrow. After lunch," she emphasized. He wasn't going to convince her to return to Hampshire Publications over a New York steak or a salad at lunch.

He smiled. She saw a little of the old Carter in that smile. A momentary flash of the man who wrestled the sheets with her burst into her mind. The same man who'd told her he was leaving and not interested in pursuing a relationship.

That was Carter Hampshire.

Carter paced the floor of his spacious apartment on Fifth Avenue overlooking Central Park. The view was spectacular, but Carter wasn't interested in it today. He punched the button on his cell phone disconnecting the call. Walking to the windows, he looked out on the traffic below. Was she down there? Renee Hart wasn't registered at the Westley Hotel. She hadn't been registered there and checked out. She'd *never* been there. Yet he'd taken her inside, seen her get on the elevator to go to her room. They'd had dinner in the restaurant last night, but she didn't have a room in that hotel. Why had she let him think she did?

Where was she?

They were supposed to meet today. Carter glanced at his watch. He wouldn't be able to meet her — he'd gotten word that his father was in the hospital and he needed to go to the Hamptons. His train left in an hour, but he hadn't been able to reach Renee. She hadn't answered her cell, and when he'd tried the hotel's number he'd been told there was no one named Renee Hart registered.

She had a wedding, he remembered. Maybe the wedding party hotel was where Renee was staying. Quickly, he went to his desk and dialed the number of the Waldorf Astoria. Renee was not registered there, either. He calmly thanked the person on the phone and disconnected.

"She lied to me," Carter said out loud. Getting up, he returned to the window. He needed to explain to her why he'd left three years ago. He'd wanted to do it last night, but the moment he'd seen her he'd known she wasn't ready to listen. So he'd tried to convince her to come back to Hampshire Publications. He wanted her there, and her job was open. When she'd been in charge, the magazine had led the industry. He knew she'd regain the share they'd lost, but she wasn't interested. Carter wanted to try and change her mind, see her again, but she'd evaded him. And now he had to go out to the Island.

He thought about how she'd looked. She was still the tall, thin woman he remembered, but there was more confidence in her appearance. And she was even more beautiful than she'd been three years ago. Her hair was black and glossy. When a curl had escaped, he'd almost reached across the table and threaded his fingers through it. Yet she'd told him he was a stranger. She couldn't know that she'd never be a stranger to him.

He was used to seeing models. Renee wasn't a model, yet her body mirrored that of the best he'd ever seen. Her waist was thin and nipped in at just the right angle. Her hips curved to exactly match the contours of his hands. Carter's fingers trembled at the thought of touching her again.

A horn sounded below. He checked the time. He had to go now or he'd never make the train. Leaving Renee another text mes-

45

sage, he left the apartment and headed for Penn Station wondering why she wouldn't take his calls and why she'd lied to him.

Renee sighed, one hand going to her breast as she studied the text message from Carter. He'd canceled their meeting. She wouldn't have to see him. Her shoulders dropped and she frowned. He hadn't said why.

Her morning meeting was over. It had been long and productive. To keep from being interrupted, she'd put her phone on silent. It had buzzed several times, but she'd ignored it. People who knew her knew she wasn't the type who instantly answered every call. With her brides, it was better to give them a little time before they reached her. By then, their crisis had been reduced to a minor problem or it had been resolved.

With nothing else to do, Renee returned to the Weddings by Diana guesthouse. The place was warm and inviting; however, it was not a place where anyone cooked. Renee had planned to have lunch before meeting Carter, and now she was hungry.

Opening the refrigerator she found only water and soft drinks. A few nonperishables were in the cabinets.

Carter had only said that something had

come up. It must have been important, she thought, as she closed the refrigerator, or maybe he'd come to his senses and realized she couldn't be persuaded to return to Hampshire Publications.

She felt deflated. She'd worked herself up for another meeting with Carter, and he'd canceled it without a reason. This was just like three years ago when he'd left with no real reason. At least today he'd sent her a text. Squaring her shoulders, Renee made a decision.

She picked her phone up from the kitchen counter. Most of the people she knew in New York also knew Carter. She wouldn't call any of them. And Blair was out of the question. Then she had an idea. She sent a text message to her cousin Dana and invited her to dinner.

Often the two cousins shared a meal while they Skyped, but Renee wished she could see Dana face-to-face.

When? Dana's reply came almost immediately. Unlike Renee, Dana was always on her phone. If she hadn't answered immediately Renee would've wondered if something was wrong.

Six o'clock, Renee texted. It didn't take long for them to work out the details. Dana loved New York and said she'd come in from

Connecticut and meet Renee at Grand Central Terminal.

She spent the afternoon catching up on email, then met Dana's train at the station. Taking a taxi, they got out of the tourist district and went to an Italian restaurant Renee was familiar with.

Dana smiled. "What's up?" She popped a fork full of lettuce into her mouth. They usually ordered salads and wine when they had these talks. But tonight Renee had ordered fettuccine Alfredo and a sangria.

"Not much," Renee said. "We haven't talked in a while. I thought it was time."

The two had grown up together and were closer than sisters. Renee had a twin brother, and she loved him, but there were things that only another woman would understand.

"So," Dana dragged the word out. A conspiratorial smile curled her lips. "Did you see Carter?"

Just like Dana to cut right to the heart. "You know, every time I come to New York you ask me that same question."

"And you evade it." Dana took another bite from her salad.

"I'm not here to see him."

"That wasn't my question," Dana said.

"He wasn't at the wedding."

"Again, not my question. Which means you saw him."

"Dinner, last night."

"Dinner! Do tell. Give me the details."

"No details. Well, one. He offered me a job."

"Back at Hampshire Publications?"

Renee heard the wonder in her cousin's voice. She took a moment to eat part of her fettuccine before nodding.

"What did you tell him?"

"That I was happy where I was."

"Are you?"

"Dana," Renee admonished.

Dana smiled slowly. "How does he look?"

"Good enough to eat."

"Well?" Dana prompted.

Renee said nothing.

Dana poked her bottom lip out like a child who wasn't getting her way.

"You can't want me to get involved with him again. After how he broke up with me. And what a basket case I was then."

Dana's face became very serious. Renee wondered if she was remembering her fiancé. He was a Marine who died in an explosion in the Middle East. Since then Dana had been alone, but she loved setting up her friends.

Dana leaned forward and said, "You

wouldn't be getting involved *again.* Because you've never gotten over him."

"That's no reason to put myself in harm's way. I've survived the last three years. I can get through the rest."

"But what about when you move back to New York? You'll be in the same city and in the same profession. It's inevitable that you'll run into each other."

"So, we'll run into each other sometimes." Renee thought it couldn't be any worse than the meeting last night. Then she'd been ambushed. Next time she'd be prepared for his possible appearance, even expecting it.

"You can handle that?"

"Sure I can." Renee's voice was strong, but she wasn't that sure of herself. She'd been tested last night, and she'd survived. It had to get easier as time went by. But even though it had been three years, her heart had jumped into her throat when she'd seen him.

She would have to weather whatever came.

"I'll be fine," Renee told Dana. "Besides, in the next few months, I'll be too busy to think of anyone. Getting a new venture off the ground is a day-and-night proposition." Renee hadn't mentioned it to Diana and Teddy, but she wanted to launch in six months.

Dana gave her a long look, then dropped her eyes. "What's happening with the new magazine?"

Her cousin had been the first person Renee had called when the project had been approved.

"Oh, good progress. And I found a place to live."

"Where?"

"It's a house. Not an apartment. And it's in the museum district."

"How'd you do that?" Dana's brows rose.

"Remember my Aunt Olivia?" Renee asked.

"Vaguely."

"She lives in the museum district."

"You're going to live with her?" Dana frowned.

Renee didn't answer immediately. She knew Dana was trying to determine Aunt Olivia's age. She was a spry eighty-three-year-old.

"You were never a favorite of hers, if I'm remembering correctly," Dana added.

Renee smiled. "She mellowed after I started working at Hampshire. I used to visit her often."

"And now you're moving in with her?" Dana's voice showed incredulity.

"Not exactly," Renee responded.

"Okay, stop dancing around and explain it to me."

"I called her a few weeks ago and she invited me to lunch. During the afternoon she told me she was leaving the city. She'd put the house up for sale but had no offers."

"Where's she going?"

"She's got a brother in North Carolina. She's going there to be near him."

"Doesn't she have children? I mean eighty-three is a hard age to pick up and move."

Renee shook her head. "She had a son. He was killed in Vietnam."

"So she's selling you the house?"

She's letting me rent it with an option to buy."

"That was lucky."

Renee nodded. "There are some legal papers I have to sign tomorrow."

Renee's cell phone rang and the photo of the caller appeared. Renee stared at it.

"Aren't you going to answer it?"

Renee said nothing. The ringing continued, causing a high-pitched whine in her ears. A sound she hadn't heard in years. It couldn't be coming from the phone, but pinging back and forth inside her brain.

"Renee, are you all right?" Dana asked.

"Who's on the phone?"

Renee lifted the small device and held it up. Dana drew in a mouthful of air.

Carter's photo stared back at her.

Renee hit Reject to stop the ringing. It rang three more times before she and Dana left the restaurant and returned to the town house.

As they stepped in the door, the ringing began again.

"You're going to have to answer it some-time. Obviously, the man is persistent," Dana said. "And it could be something important."

A hundred thoughts flashed through Renee's mind, but she couldn't pin any of them down. Why was he calling still? Why hadn't she deleted his photo from her cell phone? She hadn't seen it in three years, hadn't thought of it. It just stayed there, like some specter waiting for the perfect time to strike.

Renee pulled her phone out of her purse. She didn't hear Dana leave the room, but as she inspected the phone, Renee noticed she was alone. The phone continued its insistent ring. Renee continued to stare at it. Her finger hovered above the reject button. Then she quickly pushed Accept. She wouldn't let him intimidate her any longer.

"Carter," she said, using her happiest smile, one she did not feel.

"You deliberately deceived me about where you were staying," he began without a hello.

"I did," she admitted. She heard him swallow. He obviously wasn't expecting her to admit the truth.

"Why?"

"It's a privacy thing. I didn't want to be disturbed."

"I disturb you?"

She saw the shadow of a smile on his lips.

"Not in the way you're thinking," Renee told him. "And you canceled our meeting today. So we're even."

"I had to cancel the meeting. My father is in the hospital. I had to come out to the Hamptons."

"Oh," she said. "I'm sorry. Is he going to be all right?"

"They're still doing some tests, but you know my dad. He's a powerhouse. And he's not as bad as my mother made me believe."

Renee knew Joseph and Emily Hampshire — Joseph had run the magazine empire for years. He was a fair man and loved by his employees. She liked him a lot. His wife, Emily, was a fashion designer, and she could be excitable. Having a sick husband qualified as a good reason.

"Please let him know he's in my thoughts," Renee said.

"He'll like that. He always liked you," Carter said. "When I get back, I want to reschedule our meeting."

"Carter, we had a chance three years ago. You chose to end it. I've moved on with my life, and I suggest you do the same."

"I didn't call you to rekindle a love affair."

Renee took a deep breath. She felt a knife slip into her heart. They hadn't had an affair, and the love had only been on her side. "Then why are you calling?"

"We talked about a position at Hampshire last night. You were supposed to give me an answer tonight."

"I respectfully decline," she said.

"Respectfully?" he questioned. "Are we going to be that formal?"

"It's considered good manners to be formal with people you've just met. Remember, we are strangers."

"Oh, right. We're strangers. So, if we are strangers, then why don't we act like we just met and we can discuss my offer like adults?"

"We've already discussed it, and I'm happy with my current position."

"I hear you have a house."

Renee gulped. How could he know that? She hadn't even told Blair.

"I guess that means you're moving back to the city permanently."

Did she hear hope in his voice? Did she want to hear it? Renee mentally shook herself. Carter didn't want her, only her expertise in the bridal industry.

"I'll be working and living here. But, like I said, I'm keeping the position I have. And how did you know?"

"So, you're not leaving town as you said."

"No," she answered. And you didn't tell me how you knew."

"My mother told me."

"Your mother?" Renee frowned.

He nodded. "My mother designs for Lealia Sauvageau. She and her husband own the house next to the one you bought."

"I recognize Lealia Sauvageau's name," Renee said. "What does she got to do with this?"

"She'd ordered a gown from my mother and would no longer need it since she and her husband have sold their house and are moving. In the course of conversation, Lealia told my mom that the house next to them was being rented by a bridal magazine owner."

"And you naturally thought I was the only owner of a bridal magazine in town?"

"Naturally," he replied. "Especially since you're the only one coming from Princeton."

Renee closed her eyes.

"Small world," she said flatly.

"Isn't it? Lealia thought she was helping my mom by giving her a lead for another place to showcase her designs."

"I see."

"Anyway, now that you're going to be here, we can have that dinner tomorrow night. It'll be a small celebration, marking your return to New York."

"Carter, I'm very busy and we've already met for lunch once. We don't need to prolong this . . ." She didn't know what to call it. It wasn't friendship.

"You're not afraid of being across a table from me, are you?" he interrupted.

She laughed. "You're not going to play the fear card. You know I have no fear where you're concerned. But I decide who I want to eat with and that has nothing to do with you laying down a challenge."

"So the answer is . . ."

Renee weighed the invitation for a long time. She saw Dana in the doorway gesturing for her to accept. Dana could only hear one side of the conversation, but she could tell Carter had asked to see Renee. Renee knew it was best to stay away from him, but if she was going to live in New York and inevitably run into him, she would have to become comfortable in his presence.

"Fine," she said. "Dinner tomorrow."

"You're not going to stand me up, are you?"

"I keep my word," she said.

"Where are you staying?" he asked.

Renee was not about to give him the address. She knew he often showed up early for a date, and then they wouldn't make it out.

"You discovered I'm renting a house, yet you don't know where I'm staying." She paused, then said, "I'll meet you at the Rainbow Room at seven."

She heard his sigh through the phone. "Rainbow Room it is."

"Tomorrow, then."

"Good night, Renee."

She clicked the end button without saying anything. The tone of his voice with those three words had taken away her power of speech. Did he know he was doing that? Was it on purpose, designed to throw her off guard? She'd heard those words in the dark, after a fervent night of lovemaking. They'd wrapped around her, folded her in a blanket of warmth, the way his arms had. She'd voluntarily gone there, taken his hand and run with him into an unknown place that held the promise of forever.

Renee had never wanted to leave it. She'd wanted to see the next bend, open the next door and find what surprises awaited her. She'd wanted to jump from cloud to cloud and go with the man of her dreams.

In his arms, she had been blinded. She'd forgotten that dreams have the permanence of smoke. And it had blown up in her face. The relationship had hardly begun before the burning between them had been doused, leaving only smoke and cinders. It had taken her a while to get herself under control, to not open her eyes in the morning and find herself thinking of him. But she was at that point now. And there was no way she was allowing him back into her heart.

CHAPTER 3

Renee took a deep breath and stepped off the elevator on the 65th floor of Rockefeller Center. She wore a formfitting red dress with shoes that sparkled. It had taken her a while to decide what to wear. This wasn't a date, she kept telling herself. But who goes to the Rainbow Room just to eat? Then she decided to throw caution to the wind and dress as well as she could. She'd show Carter what he was missing and then not let him touch it.

Carter was standing by the door when she arrived. He smiled, looking her over.

"I should have worn sunglasses," he said, his smile wide. "You're dazzling."

Renee couldn't help returning it. "Thank you."

He didn't wink at her, but the slight change in his eyes told her he approved. The thought warmed her in places she wished it didn't. He reached to give her a hug, and Renee steeled herself. She stopped him before he could pull her into his arms.

"Still strangers?" he asked.

"Good evening, Carter." Renee ignored his question. He was dressed in a black suit with a gleaming white shirt and shoes that had a mirror shine. The man could be a GQ model instead of a publishing magnate.

"Your table is ready," the maître d' said.

Renee followed the black-coated man to a table for two next to the large windows that looked out on the city. The night was clear, giving them a panoramic view of the Empire State Building and Washington Square Park.

For a while, Renee buried her face in her menu. She knew what she wanted, but spent time looking over the selections as if she were deciding. She was avoiding looking at Carter, and now that they were here, she wondered what they had to talk about. It couldn't be their past.

"Are you hiding?" Carter asked.

She closed the menu and laid it on the side of the table. "I was checking over the new entrées. It's been a while since I was here."

For a moment he only stared at her. Renee stifled a smile. She'd accomplished her goal. Carter gazed at her with appreciation, and she could see a glimmer of attraction in his eyes.

A waiter brought them a bottle of champagne and went through the ritual of opening and pouring the wine into flutes. Taking their order, he quietly disappeared. Carter raised his glass and Renee clinked hers with it, the bell sound of the crystal rang clear.

"Congratulations," he said.

"On what?" Renee asked.

"Your move."

"I haven't moved yet."

"Tell me about the new house. Where is it?"

"It's up in the museum district." She avoided giving him a specific address. It wasn't like he'd show up on her doorstep, but if she was going to keep her heart intact, she wanted him to know as little about her as possible.

"Will you be launching your magazine from there?"

Their food arrived, and she took a moment to take a bite and swallow before answering. "Now that I've secured living space, I'm looking for offices for the magazine."

"So you'll be back for a site search."

Renee felt the color creep under her skin. She'd walked into that. "I will."

"When?"

"I have no current plans."

"Will you let me know when you return?" he asked straight out.

"No," she said without hesitation.

"Why not?"

"I'm not here to see you. When I come, my time will be limited. As you've said, launching a new magazine takes a lot of work."

"So you're not dating." He stated it as a fact.

The switch in subject gave her whiplash. "My love life is not your concern," she told him. "And yours is no concern of mine, but why is it you're here with me instead of being out with some other woman? As I remember, you never had a problem getting dates. I don't imagine that has changed."

"I'm between women at the moment."

Renee took a bite of her food, but she regretted it the moment she put it in her mouth. She was sure she couldn't swallow it. Yet the fact that he was unattached caused a small flutter in her stomach.

"What about you? Married? Divorced? Is there someone back in New Jersey waiting for you?" Carter asked.

"Not married, not divorced. If you're asking if I'm dating, yes," she lied.

There was no one special back in Princeton. There were men she knew, and if she needed a date, she'd have no trouble getting one. But there was no one she'd run to with good or bad news.

"Anyone special?" Carter persisted.

"You're getting really personal," Renee said.

He sat back as if he was backing off. "I apologize. It's just been a long time since we've seen each other. I was only trying to catch up."

"I see." Renee said it slowly. She put her fork down and folded her arms along the edge of the table. "I have a question I've been dying to ask for three years," she said.

Carter didn't hesitate, but Renee could see the change in him. He must have known what was coming. "Go ahead," he said.

"What happened three years ago? I felt like we were going along smoothly, then the floor fell away and there was nothing holding me up."

"It was timing, Renee. It just didn't work."

"Well, answer this, then. What's changed in the past three years that you want to be in my company now?"

The air around their table grew instantly heavy and despite the conversation of the other diners, the room felt utterly quiet.

"Nothing's changed," Carter said. And he meant it. He still felt the same way about Renee as he had when he left to go to Afghanistan.

Carter had known this question would come sometime. When he'd left there had been no guarantee that he would return, and he'd wanted to save Renee from what could happen. Three years ago it had seemed like the right thing to do. But tonight, as he looked at her beautiful face and the way her body moved in that red dress, he wasn't so sure.

He had to tell her, but not right now.

"Do you mind if we postpone that question until the end of the night? I will explain, but I don't want to start the evening with that."

Renee nodded. Carter could tell this was not the response she was expecting. But he needed more time to decide how to tell her.

"What's it like working as a consultant?" he asked, hoping to lighten the mood.

Renee leaned back and seemed to relax. The tension bunching the muscles in the back of his neck relaxed.

"It's the other side of the table," she said. "Working directly with the people who buy the gowns we put in the magazines gave me a totally new perspective on what they want and how to please them."

"Do you like that side of the business?"

She nodded. "Like any job, it has its good and bad moments. For the most part, they were good," she said. "I love the gowns, and I love seeing the glow on the brides' faces when they see themselves for the first time in white lace or satin. Often the emotions surprise them so suddenly that tears spill down their faces. That's something we can't duplicate in the pages of a bridal magazine."

"Is that what you want to do?" Carter asked. "Return to the magazine world so you can infuse emotion into the pages?"

Renee seemed to take a moment to ponder that. "Yes," she said, speaking in a whisper. Her face showed she'd hadn't thought of it until that moment. "I like production and development. I like layout and finding new ways of presenting the designs. Otherwise, I wouldn't be about to launch a magazine."

"But now you know what you want to do to make this one different from the crowd of bridal issues already on the newsstands."

"I suppose I shouldn't have admitted that to you. After all, we are going to be in competition with each other."

"I promise to keep your secret." He leaned forward as if they were conspirators. "And that's only one idea. As much as I'd like to know more, I can't get in your head and see what else is in there."

Renee swallowed. He could tell she knew there was a double meaning in his words. Carter had fallen for her the moment Blair introduced them. He hadn't understood the attraction. It was much too fast, and he'd never had any feelings as immediate as those before.

Resisting them seemed the natural thing to do. But he'd found himself taking more interest in the bridal division. His eyes were always on her when they were in a room together. He loved talking to her, sharing opinions. But then he'd had to leave, and making her play the waiting game would have been unfair.

A burst of song came from another room. Both of them glanced toward the door.

"It's a wedding," Renee said.

"Ever crash one?" Carter asked.

"I never needed to."

She smiled and Carter felt the warmth of it. This was the first time she'd really smiled at him. The others had been imitations, put on at the right time, but not genuine. This one was, and he wished he could capture and hold it.

"Wanna crash this one?"

"You're not serious?" she whispered as if the entire wedding party could hear her.

"Come on." Carter stood, holding his hand out.

"We haven't finished eating," she told him.

"The food will wait."

Renee put her hand in his. He wanted to hold her, and slow dancing at a wedding would give him an excuse.

"We'll be right back," he told the waiter as they headed for the reception.

"Hi, Renee, I didn't know you were going to be here."

"Hello," she said to Roni, a wedding consultant from one of the New York companies. "We're only here for a dance." Renee looked at Carter. "Roni, this is Carter Hampshire. Carter meet Veronica Edmonson. She's a wedding consultant for a company here. We met a couple of years ago."

They shook hands and exchanged pleasantries.

"We won't be long," Renee said.

Carter turned Renee into his arms. They began slowly moving to the music. "Do you know everyone in the business?" he asked.

"Not everyone, but it helps to know people. You never know when you'll need a favor."

Her lips were close to his ear as she said that. A tremor went through him, and his arm around her waist tightened, pulling her intimately close to him. Taking a slow breath, he inhaled her scent, felt the softness of her body and forgot everything except how good it was to hold her again.

They stayed for three more dances. The last one was slow and Carter hummed the song in Renee's ear. She couldn't help closing her eyes and giving herself up to the moment. At the end of the dance, Carter kept his arm around her back as they returned to their dinner table. Renee missed dancing with him. She missed everything about Carter, although she wouldn't admit it to anyone. She wanted to relax in his arms, melt into him and let the music take them away, but that was dangerous. And she was unsure of Carter's goals. He obviously had a reason for insisting that she spend time with him. On the surface it was to get her back at Hampshire Publications, but while he had his arms wrapped around her, she wasn't sure.

"That was fun," Carter said, holding her chair as she sat.

Renee noticed his voice was deeper.

"We should do it more often," he continued.

The promise of a future together was in his words. She suppressed the excitement that rippled in her heart, but she didn't miss his tone. It was that midnight-in-the-dark sexy voice that once wrapped her in its sound. Only now they weren't alone in the dark together, because Carter had dumped her. Without a reason. He'd only said it wasn't working for him and he was moving on. So why was he here now? Why had he insisted that she have dinner with him? Was he trying to wear her down, hope they could pick up where they had left off three years ago?

She guessed he'd had plenty of women who had filled her position for longer than she had had it. She frowned, wondering what he could want. It had to be something. Renee wondered if it was the business. Did he not want her to succeed at her magazine? Could he be that petty? Quickly she dashed that idea. Carter was honorable. At least, in everything except his relationship with her.

They spent a couple more hours over dinner, talking and laughing, although she was careful of what she said. She didn't want to reveal anything that could come back to haunt her. And she continued trying to discover his motives for wanting to be in her company. There had to be something going on.

Finally it was time to leave. Renee preceded him from the dining room into the hall. She wasn't looking forward to sharing the intimacy of a taxi, but she knew Carter wouldn't let her go home alone. As they stood waiting for an elevator, a happy couple joined them. The man swung the obviously inebriated woman around in a dance move as they laughed. Renee thought she'd seen them on the dance floor. However, as spacious as the hall was, the couple bumped into Renee and Carter.

"Excuse me," the woman said, backing away and continuing to giggle.

Renee barely acknowledged her. Her attention was on Carter. He'd grabbed her around the waist to steady her and she was now in his arms. Heat flashed through her. She trembled against him but pushed herself away as the doors of two elevators opened simultaneously. Rushing into the small sanctuary, she took a deep breath and Carter followed her in.

"Should I apologize?" Carter asked as they began the descent to street level.

Renee didn't pretend to misunderstand him. She shook her head.

71

Carter stood next to her and took her hand. Electricity skidded up her arm, but she didn't let go.

The taxi ride to the East Side was short and they spent it in silence. At the guesthouse, Renee opened the car door.

"You don't have to get out," she said. "It'll be hard getting another taxi in this area."

She slid out. Carter didn't take her advice. He got out, too, but he asked the driver to wait.

At the town house's door, he surveyed the facade and asked, "Is this yours?"

"No," she said without further explanation.

"Who lives here?"

"No one."

"No one?" His brows rose.

"I'm using it temporarily."

"Until when?" Carter persisted.

"Until I go back to Princeton."

He stared at her, waiting.

"Carter, I enjoyed dinner. Thank you for asking me." She sounded like some high school student from a B movie.

"I did, too."

Renee made the mistake of looking up at him. She wanted to know if he was being sincere. His eyes connected with hers in the low light of the outside bulb. She couldn't look away. She couldn't stop herself from watching his head come down toward her and his lips settle on hers. She pulled away almost immediately.

"What's wrong?"

"We are. We've done this before, and we know it doesn't work."

"We don't know that."

"Should I refresh your memory?" Renee asked. "I can recite the words for you. You told me point blank and to my face. 'I don't love you.' Then you disappeared, and I didn't hear from you again."

Putting her hand on the doorknob, she stared at him. The indication was that he should leave. Carter stood his ground, and a staring war ensued between them.

Renee didn't move when Carter finally took a step. She was ready to push the door open and go inside. Before she could twist the knob, his hands imprisoned her and his mouth seared hers. She couldn't do anything captured between his body and the wall, both as solid and unforgiving as granite.

She tried to resist his mouth, but her resolve wasn't strong enough. She melted into him, joining him in the kiss and letting go of all thought. Her eyes fluttered close and she clung to him, lifting herself higher on her toes.

He lifted his mouth, yet their lips still touched. She could taste him as he stared into her eyes. Then he removed the millimeter of space and kissed her again. This time his mouth was questioning, asking if it was all right to go on. His lips brushed hers, sweeping back and forth with a touch so light it was disconcerting. Renee turned as his arms gathered her closer, spanning her waist and sides. Without thinking, she went up on her toes, pressing her mouth closer to his. Her arms circled his neck and he crushed her against him for the second time. It had been too long since she'd felt like this. No one had held her or kissed her or made her feel as loved as Carter Hampshire.

She knew this was wrong. She shouldn't do this. She and Carter had no future. There was a time when they could have had a relationship, but when they'd reached that fork in the road, they'd stumbled. Still she couldn't deny herself the pleasure of being in his arms. Carter swept his tongue into her mouth. Shockwaves of emotion ran the full length of her body. She felt her leg rising, brushing against his pants leg.

Then, like a splash of ice water, she remembered where she was and what she was doing. She pulled her mouth away from him and stepped out of his arms.

Carter looked down at her. The dim light from the street lamp was bright enough to show the desire in his eyes. Renee was sure her mouth was swollen from the aftermath of his invasion, a wanted invasion.

"Carter," she whispered. She could manage no other words.

"Good night, Renee." He stepped down to the street and got back in the taxi.

Renee opened her clutch, and if her keys hadn't been immediately visible she was unsure if she would have been able to find them. Or slip them into the lock and open the door.

She stepped inside and turned to look at Carter. Neither waved or said a word. She closed and locked the door and heard the taxi drive away. Looking out the side window, she watched as the cab bore Carter Hampshire out of her life for the second time.

Carter's family had a house in the Hamptons and a summer home in North Carolina, but he lived in a two-level apartment on Fifth Avenue, where one room was dedicated to music and entertainment. Pulling his tie aside, he unbuttoned his collar

75

and took the stairs two at a time to get to the music room.

A wall unit held his CDs and an enviable collection of LPs and vinyl records. There were times when only the original medium would do. He hunted through the LPs. Renee was on his mind. She could no longer say they were strangers. After that kiss on her doorstep, there was no doubt in his mind that they were more than familiar with each other.

Fire and Desire, a Rick James favorite, was what he was looking for. Finding the album that contained the track, he placed it on the turntable and listened as the sound of love filled the cavernous room. Lowering the lights, he looked out on the city toward East 65th Street where he'd left Renee.

He wondered what she was doing. Had she changed from the red dress she wore into something sheer enough to see through? He imagined her lying on the bed, her skin tone contrasting with the white sheets. The thought aroused him.

The song ended, and Carter used his remote control to start it again. He listened to it play seven times before finally turning the machine off and heading for his bedroom.

Carter replayed their kiss over and over in

his mind. It was the last thing he thought of before sleep claimed him. But his sleep was fitful. Dreams of Renee filled the night. She wasn't pliable in his arms, but pulling away, eluding him and running whenever he tried to catch her.

Waking with a headache, he swung his legs to the floor and hung his head. Light filtered through the sheer curtains and hurt his eyes. Going to the bathroom, he found some headache medicine and downed two white pills. Thirty minutes later, he was dressed for work. His headache had only abated slightly.

The coffee timer pinged as he walked into the kitchen. He poured a cup and picked up his cell phone. It might be early, but he remembered that Renee was an early riser. He dialed her number. The phone went straight to voice mail, but the recording told him she was not accepting calls at this time.

"Damn," he cursed. If he couldn't wake up with her by his side, he at least wanted to talk to her on the phone.

Taking a sip of his coffee, he wondered if she was already on the train back to Princeton. She hadn't said when she'd return, and she had told him she would not contact him when she did. But that should all have changed last night outside her front door.

He hadn't answered her question, Renee thought as the train rolled toward Princeton. He'd never told her the reason he'd left, like he'd promised he would.

Then there was the kiss at her door. That had rendered her unable to think clearly. All she'd wanted after that was to get on one side of the door and leave him on the other. This weekend had been a test, and according to her own standards, she'd failed.

There was no available taxi at the Princeton train station when Renee arrived. By the time she walked the short distance to Nassau Street, she had a plan. She wouldn't see Carter again. Getting the magazine up and running would consume her for several months. Any invitations that included him, she'd refuse. Any calls from him, she'd ignore.

Renee sighed as she entered her home. It felt good to be back, welcoming, even though no one was there. She'd be moving out soon, but not selling. She'd decided to rent the house. Princeton was a college town and there were always people looking for residences. Mentally, Renee kept planning, forcing her mind to remain on tasks instead of thinking about the weekend and Carter.

She'd barely gotten unpacked before the phone at her computer rang. The signal told her it was a Skype call. Renee knew it was Dana calling to find out how the weekend had gone.

"Hi, Dana," she said cheerily.

"How was it?" Dana replied.

"Dinner was fine. The food at —"

"I'm not interested in the food," Dana interrupted. "How did it go with you and Carter?"

"As it always did," she replied.

Dana smiled. "Really?"

"It's not what you think. We had a normal dinner and spoke like friends."

"Friends!" Dana's face fell. "I thought you two might mend some fences."

"Why? Why would you think that?"

"Renee, this is me. Dana. I know you're still in love with him. You've been that way since time began."

"That's not true," she began. "We weren't together long enough for that."

Dana, raising her finger, stopped Renee from continuing. "It only takes a moment," Dana said. "Some relationships can take years to develop and others can happen in the blink of an eye."

Or a glance, Renee thought. "Well, it usually takes two people to make a relationship."

"Do you think he wants one?"

Renee frowned. "I'm not sure. He wants something. I could feel it each time we've met, but he hasn't really said what it is. For sure he'd like me to return to Hampshire Publications, but I'm committed here and I have no intention of returning there."

"Well, be careful. I don't want you to be hurt again."

Renee smiled.

"So, when are you moving?"

Renee sat up in her chair and relaxed her shoulders. The change in subject removed a weight from them.

"Next month, after Aunt Olivia moves out. I have to have her house cleaned and painted, get a manager for this house and hire a moving company, plus pack while planning the magazine."

"A plateful, I see."

"Isn't it always like that?"

Both she and Dana thrived on keeping busy and getting things done. As teenagers, Dana had visited Renee wherever her father was stationed.

"When you do move, I'll come to the new house and help you unpack."

"Thanks, I'd love the company."

Renee's cell phone rang and she glanced toward it, but it was too far away for her to see the caller ID.

"I guess people know you're home," Dana said. "I have to go anyway. Talk to you again soon."

Dana disconnected the call. The cell continued to ring. Renee expected it to be Carter. She took a deep breath and stood up. If it was him, she'd ignore the call.

Lifting the phone, she turned it over.

Teddy's face appeared in the small window.

CHAPTER 4

Three weeks later, Renee was back in New York. She'd heard nothing from Carter in all that time, and she was beginning to think things were settled between them. Yet the memory of her performance in his arms outside of the guesthouse wasn't as easy to put behind her.

"I have a wonderful place for you to see," her real estate agent, Eloisa, told her. "It's within your budget, centrally located and immediately available."

Renee had been searching for office space for a week with little result. There was plenty of property available, but everything had at least one problem that made it unsuitable. When she saw a place that would work, the contract had clauses that were deal breakers.

She met Eloisa down the block from the next space they were viewing, and they walked toward the building together. But she resisted when Eloisa pulled open the glass door and waited for her to enter a building Renee was so familiar with she could navigate it blindfolded.

"Is something wrong?" Eloisa asked.

Renee moved to the side, stepping out of the flowing sea of humanity moving around her. "This is the Hampshire Building," she said. Her voice was quiet, the kind of quiet that showed desperation. Renee wasn't angry. Eloisa hadn't known. It was almost like her words were an explanation to herself, to calm her down.

"They have wonderful offices and the space is available."

"But Hampshire Publications has a bridal division and my magazine caters to that market. We'll be in competition with each other."

The likelihood of running into Carter in an elevator or on the street increased tenfold if she even considered this space.

"I checked the contracts and there is no exclusion related to other magazine publishers."

"But it's unethical," Renee said.

Eloisa inclined her head in a gesture of surrender. "I can find you other spaces to consider," she said, "but they'll likely have a higher rent."

"Let's look at them," Renee said. Even though she was tired of looking, tired of negotiating and tired of discovering unsuitable locations, she would continue the search.

Two weeks passed, and finally Eloisa confronted her. "We've been everywhere. I'm at a loss to find you anything unless you increase your price point or your location."

Renee wished she could, but she had a budget and she had to stay within it. The Weddings by Diana partners had already been more than generous with her start-up cost estimates.

"How about we revisit the Hampshire Building?" Eloisa suggested with a happy note to her voice. "The least you could do is look at the space."

Renee nodded, but her heart sank.

Twenty minutes later they were in the office space, and Renee knew it was perfect for her needs. Very little renovation would be necessary. Some of the items she'd budgeted for were already present.

"What do you think?" Eloisa asked after a long while.

"It's perfect," Renee said without enthusiasm.

"Great." Eloisa didn't inject any excitement into the word. "Does that mean you'll take it?"

Renee looked at her. She nodded, unable to speak. All she could think of was that Carter Hampshire was only twenty floors above her. Thankfully, she'd noticed that the set of elevators that serviced her floor was different than the ones that went to his. They weren't even in the same hallway. She wouldn't run into him if she was lucky.

But where Carter was concerned, luck had never been on her side.

Numbers don't lie, Carter thought. It was a mantra his father had taught him when he was showing him the business. And Carter didn't like the numbers he was seeing. He was going to have to do something about it soon.

He heard a tap on his door. "Come in," he called.

Blair opened the door and smiled as she walked into his office.

"What's new?" she asked. "You usually like to come down and walk through the office."

Carter did. Instead of asking his division heads to come to his office, he'd go to their offices. That way, he could smile at the staff and get to know them. Again, this was

85

something his father had taught him and Carter continued to do it. It was also how he had first met Renee.

Suddenly, she walked into his mind and filled it with her presence. He imagined her standing in the middle of the conference room. She was talking and the glass wall allowed him to fully stare at her.

"Carter," Blair called him, doing the same thing now that she'd done years ago.

"I've been looking at the reports on the bridal division," he said.

"We've had a setback, but we discussed that. We'll bounce back."

Carter stood up and walked around the office. "Do you think so?"

"What?" she asked. "Do you think Renee can have that much impact on the market with a small magazine?"

"It's not Renee. Her magazine hasn't launched yet, despite all the buzz in the air. But we've been losing market share for some time now. If we don't get sales up, I'm going to have some very bad reporting to do."

"It's the market," Blair stated. "The number of weddings is down, so we won't have the same number of brides looking for magazines."

"The number of weddings is actually up,"

Carter corrected her. "I thought that might be the reason, but after getting the statistical reports, I found the opposite to be true."

"Well, we'll just have to come up with a campaign to put us back on track."

Carter didn't smile. "That will be a start," he said. "But we'll have to keep it up issue after issue. Confidentially, we've now begun losing money on this division. If we don't turn it around, we'll have to put it up for sale or close it."

"You're not serious," Blair said. The surprise was genuine on her face.

"I've been covering for the sales for a while. I can't keep operating the division without it holding its own."

Blair looked directly at him, although she remained in her seat. "I guess we'll have to come up with something so irresistible to the bridal market that they have to buy it. But don't worry. I have an idea or two up my sleeve."

Moving day was never easy. Renee knew that from the many times she'd moved with her family. Her father was in the military, and every couple of years they'd pull up stakes and relocate, most times to another country. The army had packed and shipped their things, but her mother insisted on unpacking and putting everything away, along with the help of her twins, Renee and her brother, Roger. During summers, Dana would come and stay with her until school started. They'd had some of the best times of their lives those summers.

Renee's new house was filled with boxes, and she could barely walk around. But instead of completing her home move, she was focusing on setting up her new office space. Everything and everyone was there at the same time: electricians, the phone company, furniture deliveries. So much for an orderly move. The place was chaos central. The only person who wasn't there was Carter, and she had to be thankful for that. He was twenty floors above her and she hoped she could avoid him for the rest of her life.

The sun had set ages ago, and finally the place had some semblance of order. She didn't worry about organizing her office as long as the heavy pieces, like her desk and cabinets, were in place. The other areas of the office space had desks and equipment. She was also in the process of hiring people to fill those spaces.

There was a small kitchen along the opposite wall from her office. Renee headed there to make herself a cup of coffee. Even though the sun had gone down, she had hours to go before heading to her new home, where an equally chaotic bedroom awaited her. She wasn't planning to open anything there tonight.

"Do you mind if I have one of those?"

Renee jumped at the sound. Twirling around she saw a thin woman with long red hair standing in the doorway. Renee had seen her most of the day, directing and helping with the placement of furniture.

"I'm sorry. I thought everyone from the moving company had gone."

Renee poured a second cup of coffee and handed it to her. "Milk is in the fridge and sugar on the counter."

The woman smiled and added milk and one sugar to her cup. She turned back to Renee.

"You don't have to stay after you finish your coffee," Renee told her. "I can handle things from here."

"I'm not with the moving company," the woman said. She smiled as if she had a secret. "I'm Wanda Guilliard, your three o'clock."

"My interview! I totally forgot." Renee stood up straight. "I am so sorry." She looked at her watch. It was nearly seven o'clock. "Why didn't you stop me?"

"You were so busy and you looked like you really needed help." Wanda looked through the kitchen door at the chaos that was still in the outer rooms. "When I arrived, a man thrust a box at me and said to put it over there." She indicated one of the offices.

"But you worked all afternoon. I saw you and I thought you were with the movers. I did wonder why you were wearing a skirt, but only in passing."

"I was dressed for an interview. But I had walking shoes in my tote bag, so I changed into them." She put a foot out and Renee looked at the tennis shoes.

She laughed. Wanda joined her. "I can't thank you enough. If you work as well with the computer as you did with the move, the job is yours."

"I am qualified," she said.

Renee gestured for her to sit down. They both moved to one of the two round tables.

"I have a degree from Columbia. I studied design and business, and I can show you my portfolio of other publications I've designed. I can break down and troubleshoot the insides of a computer and I'm fluent enough in Microsoft Office to teach."

"How are you at digital publishing?"

"I know it cold."

"You're very confident," Renee said. Despite her selling herself so hard, Renee liked her. Even if Wanda could only do half of what she professed, she would fit in. Renee had managed before and she knew that if someone didn't work out, she would terminate them.

"I don't mean to be overbearing. I can do what I say and probably more. It just depends on what you need."

"I need someone who can run the digital design side of the business. We will produce a full print issue each month, and I need someone to lay out the pages so they can be sent to a printer for the final product."

"I'm sure that won't be a problem," Wanda said.

"Have you ever worked for a magazine before?"

Wanda shook her head. "I'm currently employed at Parks, Kagen and Cooper, a law firm in Jersey City."

"What do you do there?"

"I run their website. And before you ask, I'm looking for something more challenging."

"I'm sure we can fill that bill," Renee commented.

"How many people will be in the production and design department here?"

"Right now, there's only you."

"Does that mean I have the job?" Wanda bit her bottom lip.

Renee smiled. "If the salary meets your requirements." Renee told her what she'd budgeted.

"We're good," Wanda said. "When do I start?"

"You tell me. We have to do a background check. And I suppose you need to notify the law firm of your decision."

"Two weeks will work for me," Wanda told her.

"By then I'll have this mess in order." Renee smiled again. She liked Wanda. Apparently, she was a pitch-in-when-and-where-needed type of person. And Renee needed someone like her.

"If you don't mind, I'd like to help with the computer setup and arrangement," Wanda said. "I want to make sure all the programs I need are properly installed and ready for use."

Designed for Brides officially had its first employee. Wanda wasn't afraid to get her hands dirty, and she didn't ask for much direction. She was exactly the kind of person Renee had hoped to find.

One down, seven to go, Renee thought when Wanda waved good-night. Renee went around turning out the lights and locking up the place. She'd be in the next day to continue putting things in order. One office at a time, she told herself.

She left the building by a rear exit and walked around to the front heading for the subway.

"Renee." Carter's voice stopped her. She'd reached the curb and was waiting for the light to change.

A shudder went through her at both the sight of him and the way he said her name. She glanced over her shoulder, hoping there was someone or something there that would give her an excuse to get away from him quickly. Nothing materialized. Her day had been long, and she wanted nothing more than to grab something to eat and take a long bath before going to bed.

"Late day?" he asked.

She nodded.

"Just going to pick up something and go home," she answered.

"I was about to get something to eat. Why don't you join me?"

"I'm a little tired. I think I'll just go home."

"Renee, you have to eat. And it's only a quick bite together, not a full dinner. Although we could go to dinner if you wish . . ."

"I'm just going to pick something up, but thank you. Good night." She darted across the street and buried herself in the crowd.

In front of her was her favorite deli, but she walked by it. There was another one on the next corner and she'd rather not have Carter following her inside a place so close to the office. There was a traffic jam of people already standing in line to order something to eat before heading home, and Renee joined the crowd. She could cook her own dinner, but she was too tired. Her back and neck hurt and doing nothing when she got home was her goal.

Placing her order, Renee stepped back. She bumped into someone and instinctively turned to apologize.

"I'm sorry," she said. Then she saw who it was. "Carter, what are you doing here? I thought you'd spend your dinner hour in a fancy restaurant with the opposite sex."

"And look at you, the bridal wizard, fulfilling every woman's dream of grabbing a sandwich and a drink and taking it back to your lonely kitchen."

"You don't know that," Renee said.

"Don't I?"

The clerk called her order. It was obviously a sandwich for one. Renee took it, paid and left, hoping to get away from Carter before his order was ready.

He caught up with her before she could find a cab. Without asking, he took her arm, hailed a passing taxi and pushed her inside.

"Where are we going?" she asked.

"Your place," he said.

She leaned back, her eyebrows raised.

"Would you rather go to my place?" He leaned forward and put his hand on the latch of the connecting window.

"No!" she stated too quickly and too loudly.

Renee gave her address and Carter slid the window back in place.

He relaxed, leaning back in the seat and sighing.

"Bad day?" Renee asked.

"A little more than usual."

"Wanna talk about it?" Renee regretted her words as soon as she said them.

Carter looked at her. Both of them remembered when they'd worked together. When he'd had a bad day or she'd had one, they would always vent about it together.

That was how it had begun. Those talks at the end of the day. Soon they'd added food delivery, then picking up something and eating together, until finally dinner and making love had followed. She wasn't going down that road again. They no longer worked together, and they were no longer lovers. They weren't even friends anymore. They were rivals.

"I'll work it out," he said.

Renee wondered if he hadn't answered because it had to do with the bridal division. Her heart constricted a moment. She missed their long after-work conversations. She couldn't stop the regret that spilled out of its hiding place.

They might be colleagues, but friends they weren't. And lovers they would never be again.

Carter's week had been one crisis after another, mainly in the bridal division where two graphic artists had resigned. He barely had time for anything but the office and thoughts of Renee, whom he hadn't seen since that night in the deli.

Heading into the Hampshire Building, he wondered where Renee's offices were. They had to be close by or he wouldn't have run into her.

Carter stepped into the office elevator. For a moment his finger hovered over the buttons before he punched thirty-eight.

He'd been trying to reach her for the past two weeks. But each time he dialed her number, it went to voice mail. Obviously, she did not want to talk to him. Carter understood when no meant no. And Renee was telling him no. He'd thought that after the frank conversation about the layouts that the two of them were heading toward a new road. But something was still going on to cause her to refuse his calls.

Exiting the elevator, he spoke to pockets of people as he made his way through the hall toward his office. Two secretaries carrying cups of coffee passed him. He looked into the room where the coffee machine sat and decided to stop and get a cup.

"Good morning, Carter," Marjorie said. Marjorie worked as an assistant to the company's legal director.

"Good morning."

She poured a cup of coffee, then headed in the direction of her office.

Just before Carter reached the door to his own office in the corner he heard a name that stopped him.

"Renee Hart. I was so surprised to see her. It's been years."

Carter turned back, coffee in one hand, his briefcase in the other.

"What's she doing here? I thought she moved to New Jersey." The other woman asked.

"I don't know, but she looks like wherever she's been, it agrees with her."

"She was always beautiful. I wish I had her complexion, so smooth and clear."

They started to walk away, when Carter called out. He didn't intend to, but he heard his voice. "Sandra?"

She turned toward him as the other woman walked away.

"You saw Renee? When?"

"This morning. A few minutes ago, actually. It was strange. I got on the wrong elevator, the one that only goes to the twenty-fourth floor, and she was there. I was talking and turned into the first bank instead of the second.

"I didn't realize I'd gotten in the wrong elevator until we'd passed the sixth floor where I could switch from one bank to the other. So I rode up with her."

"Where did she get off?"

"On eighteen," she said with a sly smile.

"Thanks."

Sandra gave him a look that said she wanted to ask a question, but thought better of it. She turned and walked away. Carter went into his office and pushed the door closed.

Here? What was she doing here? Who was she visiting on the eighteenth floor? Carter put his coffee and briefcase down and opened his computer. As soon as it booted, he pulled up a list of tenants. Filtering them by floor, he checked the names of businesses and there it was. The name jumped out as if it was a viper. *Designed for Brides.* It was the only business on eighteen. She'd taken the entire floor. As the building's owner, Carter had access to other information about the tenants. Opening the file for *Designed for Brides,* he saw the space was leased to Weddings by Diana with a contract that had been signed by Renee Hart.

Renee was opening her magazine in his building. In the same place where he had his own bridal magazine's offices. Had she thought he wouldn't find out?

Carter closed the file, clicking the mouse button harder than necessary.

He wouldn't go down there. She had a right to lease the space. Her magazine was just a start-up, and there was no need to worry that it would cut into the profits of his company. Carter opened the sales figures for the previous day. Usually he started with the men's magazines, body building and car repair, but today he went straight to the bridal sales. Releasing a sigh, he checked the numbers. Sales were exactly as expected. Quickly he did a comparison of sales for the same week last month and last year. They were slightly down, but that was understandable. None of it had anything to do with her.

She hadn't launched yet, a voice inside his head gave him the logic. Sitting back in his chair, Carter stared at the screen and wondered when she planned to launch. There was nothing to worry about. Renee had been away three years, and she hadn't even been working in the industry. Three years was a lifetime in the magazine business. It didn't matter how well she'd done three years ago. It was all about who advertised in the magazine and what was happening in the bridal industry.

"Carter." His secretary poked her head in the door. "You're going to be late for the staff meeting."

Carter glanced at the clock on his desk. Grabbing his leather notebook, he stood up and headed for the conference room.

The rest of the day slogged by. He couldn't remember how many times he checked the clock. Renee was on his mind, and he wanted to go to the eighteenth floor and see if she was there. He wanted an explanation as to why she wouldn't take his calls.

But he vowed not to do it. After all, he

understood *no* when he heard it.

The office quieted down after five. Carter had done little other than wear the carpet out between his desk and the panoramic windows. He told himself he needed to catch up on the trade journals he hadn't read, but he couldn't focus. When he did finally open one, he was looking for information on Renee's new venture. Other than that small announcement in the issue he'd read a month ago, there was nothing.

"I thought I'd find you here."

Carter looked up. Blair stood in his doorway.

"You know, it's not a crime to go home before the late news is on." She walked to the front of his desk and took a seat in one of the guest chairs. "Or go down to the eighteenth floor."

"You know?" His brows rose.

"It's the talk of the building. People who used to work with her have been disappearing all day."

"Was one of them you?"

She shook her head. "I ran into her on the street the other day. I didn't know she had space in this building. We're having a drink Friday after work." Blair raised her hand, warding him off. "And this time you are *not* invited."

"I ran into her, too. Why would she take space in this building?"

"That's easy. We're located in the middle of all the services a magazine needs. We had available space. And there's not a rule against another publisher moving in."

Carter stared at her.

"I checked," Blair said.

"But why here?"

Blair smiled. She relaxed in the chair, crossing her legs and putting her elbow on her knee, while her hand supported her chin. "You think she came to be near you?"

"I don't. I think she doesn't want to see or hear from me."

Blair frowned.

"I've called her several times in the past few weeks. Her phone goes straight to voice mail and the recording says the number is not accepting messages And if she wanted to see me, all she'd have to do is go down to the sixth floor, cross over to the other elevator bank and come up."

"And she hasn't?"

He shook his head.

Blair stood and walked across to the windows. She cut quite a figure, having been a model in the past. Her hair was totally white, cut short and styled to emphasize her best features. For a woman over fifty, she had few lines on her face, even though her smile was infectious. She walked to the door of his office and turned back to look at him.

"There is one thing you probably forgot, Carter."

"What's that?"

"The elevator goes up *and* down."

Renee stretched her back. Slipping her feet out of her shoes, she stood and reached for the ceiling, extending one arm higher than the other, then reversing the exercise, air climbing to relieve stress. She'd been putting in fifteen-hour days for the last three weeks. Tomorrow would be another one.

Mentally she went over the last three weeks' accomplishments. She'd contracted with two sales forces, one to handle advertising and one to work with the various designers. Both started this week. Wanda, although talkative, had organized the computer network and tested all the machines. She was already laying out details for their debut issue.

Renee had hired a production team and a marketing director, and they were now nearly fully staffed. She turned and looked at the electronic production board that was mounted on the wall of her office. If all went well, they would launch in the spring. She smiled. Her back hurt, but she was satisfied. Night had already fallen. She shut down her computer and the board went dark.

Slowly she walked through the office turning off any unnecessary lights. By the time she'd collected her shoes and purse, only the light in reception remained illuminated. She switched it off. Gasping, her heart jumped into her throat as she saw Carter on the other side of the double glass doors. Renee's heartbeat jumped several hurdles. Her hand went to her heart and she let out a long breath.

Carter's features were distorted by the etching of the *Designed for Brides* logo on the door. The computer automatically locked the doors at six o'clock, but since Renee had stepped in view of the motion detector, a click unlocked them to let her out.

Grasping the curved handles, Carter pulled both doors open and stepped inside. Renee retreated a step.

"Welcome to New York," he said sarcastically. "I am truly surprised to find you here."

She didn't know what to say. She should have known that, with Sandra seeing her in the elevator and the number of people who had come to say hello, word would get back to Carter. But Renee thought she'd evaded him for one more day.

"Why are you here?" Carter asked, his tone almost demanding.

"The space was available and had everything I needed. And the building staff has been wonderful in helping me set things up."

"Stop talking about the staff. Why didn't you answer my phone calls?"

"Carter, let's not go through this again. If my being here is going to disturb you, I can find another location."

"You could have told me," he said. "Not only are you going into competition with one of my magazines, but you're going to do it in the same building."

"I'm not the only other publisher in this building. I'm also not the only one who publishes a magazine that competes with one of Hampshire Publications'. So you're not here to talk about my use of space. Why are you really here?"

He didn't immediately answer. "I want us to go back three years and start over."

"You know that's not possible."

"You're being literal," he told her.

"I am," she agreed. "The last three years happened. We can't pretend they didn't."

"Could we sit down?" Carter asked.

Renee looked around. Behind her was a loveseat with a coffee table in front of it. On either side of the table, facing the two seater, were individual chairs. She took a seat in one of the singles. Carter sat on the sofa close to her chair.

"If I apologize for leaving you, could we at least be friends?"

"I never said I wasn't your friend."

"You said we were strangers."

"And that's true," she said.

"Not anymore," he said. "Not after that night on your doorstep."

Renee's face flooded with heat. She was glad the lights were off. The soft glow from the hall didn't reach her features.

Renee looked at her still-bare feet. "I'd rather not talk about that night."

"Why not? Because it proved that you're not as immune to me as you wish?"

Renee took a deep breath. "You're right, Carter. I'm not immune to you. But I will not open my heart to a man who crushed it three years ago and has the gall to ask me to be his friend."

"If you won't be my friend, be my love."

Renee choked. She dropped her purse and the shoes she'd been holding. "You can't be serious," she said.

"I'm dead serious."

"Why?" Renee deliberately made her voice soft. "You're a good-looking man. There are at least ten women on the same floor as you who'd give their eyeteeth to hang on your arm. Why do you want me there?"

"Because you aren't one of the ten women on my floor."

"How do I know you're not asking this to find out what I'm doing to get this magazine off the ground?"

"You mean, to sabotage your efforts?" He didn't wait for an answer. "That's beneath you."

"You offered me a job at Hampshire Publications. Since I turned it down, this could just be another method of you getting what you want."

"It isn't," he said.

She wanted to believe him. Every fiber of her body wanted her to stand up and rush into his arms. But things had changed. Their lives were different.

"Where did you go, Carter?" Renee asked.

"War," he said.

Renee wasn't sure she'd heard him. It was a single word and her mind tried to think of something that she might have misheard, but nothing replaced the single word.

"War?" she asked.

"Afghanistan."

"You went to Afghanistan?" She leaned in a bit, then stopped.

"Two years."

Renee had no air. "Why didn't you tell me?"

"I couldn't. If I had told you, you might have waited for me until I got back, *if* I got back. It was my second tour. I'd seen guys get messed up over there. I didn't know what would happen to me. And I didn't know if things would change between us while I was gone."

Renee thought about Dana losing her fiancé. How would Renee have felt if Carter had been killed? She shuddered at the thought.

"Are you all right?"

"I'm fine," he said. "I came home without a scratch."

"What about the mental part?"

"I've been back a year. I take part in counseling returning soldiers. I think I'm all right, but sometimes the effects take time to set in. I can't guarantee that I'll always be fine, but for right now, I've been cleared of all medical issues."

"Carter, I am so sorry. I didn't know."

"Few people did. They thought I was working somewhere else. Some thought I'd had a disagreement with my father. Others thought it was you."

"Why keep it a secret?"

Carter stood up. He walked about the small space as if he were an animal and needed more than the cage he'd been assigned. He turned, stopping under the light near the door. "I didn't expect to return," he said. "I thought I was going to die."

Renee gasped as a mental picture flashed through her mind.

Moving more quickly than Renee thought he could, Carter was next to her, taking her hand. "We hadn't been together long. I thought if I asked you to wait, even if I told you where I was going, and then I died, it would make your life worse."

She snatched her hand free and stood, stepping away from him. "So you did this for me? You made a unilateral decision for *me*? You didn't give me the opportunity to think, to choose, for myself?"

"I can tell you don't agree with my decision, but it was for the best. What would you have done had I told you?"

"I'd . . ." She stopped. "I suppose we'll never know the answer to that question."

Was there a word that meant being both right and wrong at the same time? Carter asked himself as he opened the door to his apartment. It had been a mistake not to tell Renee where he was going. But Carter had known their relationship was new and soaring. He'd felt more for her after a single date than he'd ever felt for any other woman. And he'd known she was falling hard for him. But he had to go — he'd already been called. If anything had happened to him, he didn't want her feeling guilty or lost. It was better that they'd ended their relationship before it moved any further. Whether she believed him or not, he did it for her.

His phone rang. Carter pulled it out of his pocket, hoping he'd see Renee's photo. He hadn't changed it when he'd left for Afghanistan. He'd kept it with him and looked at her picture often during his two-year absence.

Carter blinked at the display. He blinked again. Renee's photo smiled back at him. It was the one she'd used on the website when she'd worked at Hampshire. It was the only one he had. The ringtone whirred again. He pushed the button for the speaker.

"Hullo." He cleared his throat, finding his voice was deeper than usual.

"Carter?"

"I'm here," he answered.

She took so long to say anything that Carter checked the display to see if she had ended the call.

"Renee, are you still there?" He heard her breathing. She was obviously struggling with something. "Where are you?"

"Across the street."

Carter walked to the window and looked down. He saw her standing in the light of a street lamp. She looked up at him. Carter dashed from the apartment and ran down the five flights of steps. He couldn't wait for an elevator. He crossed Fifth Avenue to the tree-lined median where she stood, still holding her phone to her ear.

He gazed down at her, unsure of what to say or do.

"I thought I should say something," she said.

Carter moved to stand next to her. Traffic sped by on the major road.

"Come with me." He took her arm and looked both ways. When the traffic opened, he pulled her across the street and shuttled her into his building. He didn't stop until they were inside his apartment and he'd closed the door. Carter didn't know how she knew where he lived. The few times they'd spent the night together it had been at her place.

Getting two glasses of wine, he gave her

one and they took seats. She chose a chair instead of sitting next to him on the sofa.

Renee sipped the white wine. "I came to apologize."

"I'm the one who owes you an apology," he said.

"I started walking. I walked for a long time. And I thought for a long time. I thought about your question. What would I have done, had I known. I'm not sure, but I know I would have worried that you wouldn't . . ."

She struggled for words. Carter didn't move.

"Then I found myself across the street. I wish you'd told me before you left," she said. "But the fact that you didn't is no reason for me to hold a grudge against you, especially since we're bound to run into each other from time to time."

Carter didn't allow her to get any further. Lightning propelled him across the room, and he hauled her into his arms and seared his mouth to hers.

His arms encased her, gathered her to him as his kiss deepened. Renee didn't resist. She didn't want to and knew that it was impossible. Her arms went around Carter and she melted into him.

She'd missed being kissed, held and loved. She missed the smell of him, the way his fingers threaded through her hair. The way his arms felt as they held her. Their heads bobbed from side to side as wet kisses covered her face before he returned to her mouth.

Carter brought out feelings that no one else could. She was aware of everything about him — she knew the weight of his arms, the strength of his embrace, the smell of his cologne and the unique scent that was his alone.

Carter's tongue invaded space she gladly yielded. It was like the last three years hadn't existed. And today she wanted him to go on kissing her until time stopped. It seemed she might get her wish. Carter's mouth changed, becoming gentler, more loving, so much so that the emotion flooding her system overloaded.

Carter raised his head, sliding his mouth from hers and cradling her like a baby against him. Renee's heart pounded and her breath came in short gasps. She could feel the pulse in Carter's neck. She knew she still affected him the way he affected her. Moments later he pushed her back and looked down at her. Renee's eyes opened slowly and she looked into his. They were dark and deep with desire.

Behind him Renee notice a lamp, and the light somehow recharged her brain.

"This doesn't change anything," she said, getting to her feet. "I wanted to apologize, but I didn't come here for . . . this."

"Why did you come?"

"I explained that."

He nodded. Renee inched closer to the door. "I'll go now."

"Renee?"

She stopped. She looked directly at him, not wanting Carter to think that he intimidated her.

"You can't win," he said.

"Maybe not, but it will be a worthy fight."

You can't win. Renee sat up in bed. Carter's words came back to her. Why did these revelations always come at night, disturbing her sleep? Pulling her knees to her chest, she clamped her arms around them and rocked back and forth. She hadn't been able to sleep. It was the smile — no, the smirk — on Carter's face as she'd left his apartment that kept her awake. What had Carter meant? Was she interpreting his parting words differently than he'd intended? She'd assumed he was talking about the business at first. That she couldn't win in the bridal market against a conglomerate that controlled the industry.

But the words came on the end of a passionate kiss. And the smirk, that I-know-something-you-don't look, was keeping her awake. While she'd spent hours, days, months planning for every eventuality in the business, she hadn't planned for a you-can't-win smirk from her prime competitor.

Pushing the cover aside, she swung her feet onto the floor and stood up. There was little chance of any more sleep tonight, so she might as well get up and unpack some of the boxes littering every surface of her house from the door to the back wall.

The unpacking worked until sunrise. By then she was ready to go back to bed. Unfortunately, it was time to shower and head for the office, an office where she could, at any time, find her nemesis standing on the other side of a glass door.

Renee knew taking this space wasn't the best idea. However, if she wanted a prestigious address and a place of business that was central and met all her requirements and budget, the Hampshire Building was it. It only had one drawback, which was Carter.

Work was the panacea. After several hours at the office, she no longer felt tired and she no longer thought of Carter more than three or four times a minute.

She called Wanda into her office, and the two of them spent the rest of the day developing something unique that could help when they launched the magazine. Eventually the day ended, and she headed home. In the lobby, Carter emerged from his elevator bank just as her elevator door opened. He fell into step with her near the front entrance, and the two of them passed through the building's exit at the same time. Neither spoke a word to the other, yet the look that passed between them spoke volumes.

Once she was in the crowd on the sidewalk, she decided to change her routine. She quickly lost sight of him and went to a deli in the opposite direction of the one she usually frequented. Carter must have had the same idea — she saw him the moment she walked through the door.

"In our attempt not to run into each other, we keep running into each other," he said.

"I'm beginning to think you're stalking me." She didn't really believe that, but she did wonder if he was baiting her, forcing her to remember and relive the scene that had taken place in his apartment.

Renee ordered her food. She hoped Carter would leave, but he remained and they left together, almost as if they'd planned to meet there.

"How are things going?" he asked. She knew his question was just to fill the silence. They weren't the small-talk types.

"If you mean how my magazine is coming along, it's right on schedule."

When they got to the subway station they had to part ways, and Renee turned to say goodnight.

"I suppose running into you is something I can't control," she said.

"And I'm not stalking you," he said.

"You said I couldn't win. Did you mean that you don't think I can make my magazine a success?"

Carter stepped closer to her. Leaning down, he kissed her cheek and whispered in her ear.

"Winning has nothing to do with any magazine."

As Renee turned and bounded down the subway stairs, heat radiated through her. Why did he have the ability to render her speechless? With anyone else she was articulate, intelligent and logical, but the moment Carter entered the room she became awkward and unable to formulate complete sentences.

"Maybe it wasn't about winning," she said aloud. Checking around her, no one seemed to notice that she was talking to herself.

She would win. She was unsure of what the rules were, but she would devise her own. She knew a lot about Carter, and anticipating his playbook wouldn't be that hard. The problem was that he knew hers, too.

By the time Renee got home, she was too tired to prepare a meal. But having meals at home would keep her from bumping into Carter at local delis again and again. She sighed.

So winning wasn't about the magazine. It was about them. Yet there was nothing between them. If she didn't participate in his games, there could be no outcome. And she could resist that. She'd concentrate on the magazine. She'd show him. And in the place it would hurt the most — business.

She and Wanda were planning a revolutionary change to the way brides viewed their gowns. No one had anything like it. It might take some time for her to win the game he was playing, but this one would set him back a step or two.

■ ■ ■ ■

Carter hated dinner parties, especially those given by his parents. While his father had retired from Hampshire Publications when Carter returned from Afghanistan, he still liked to keep track of the movers and shakers in the magazine business. His mother just liked entertaining. She had her own set of industry people who came to their house in the Hamptons two to three times a year. Her expertise was in the fashion business, which complemented the magazines.

Usually his mother was either trying to push someone into the spotlight or she was parading possible future daughters-in-law for his benefit. But it never worked. Carter was perfectly capable of finding his own bride, if and when he wanted one.

"Mother." Carter grasped her shoulders and kissed her on the cheek. She went into his arms and hugged him. She was short, only three inches over five feet. There was a time when she'd had hair long enough to reach her waist. He used to brush it before his younger sister took over the task and Carter grew old enough to want to play baseball instead of do girly things. Now her

119

hair was salt and pepper, and had been cut into a chic style that tapered at her neck.

"No date?" she asked instead of saying hello.

"What, and have you making wedding plans before I even get a drink?"

"I wouldn't do that," she said. "I'd wait until after you got a drink." Both of them laughed.

"I see you have quite a turnout from the city," Carter commented. "Which one have you singled out for me?" He looked over the crowd of dressed-to-the-nines females. Most people he either knew by name or recognized.

"Darling, I thought you might come with Renee Hart. I hear she's back in the trade."

"Who's back in the trade?" His father joined them. Dressed in his white tie and tuxedo, few people would know Joseph had been in the hospital recently. Thankfully, his diagnosis hadn't been very serious. However, he did need to take things easy.

"Renee Hart," his mother said.

"I liked her." His father didn't hesitate. "I could live with her."

"It wouldn't be you who would live with her," Carter told his dad. His father was the one person who knew how he felt about Renee.

"I've heard she's back," Carter said, hedging.

"Between the two of you, I'm surprised she isn't here." The look that passed between his parents told him they knew something. "She isn't here, right?"

"Right," his mother answered.

Carter let a breath out.

"But . . . she's expected," his father finished.

"I can't believe you two. I'm thirty-two, not thirteen."

"We didn't invite her just for you," his mother said. "She's an up-and-coming force in the industry. When she worked for you, she was invited. It would be a slight not to invite her now that she's back in the industry."

There were other competitive publishers in the room, and while Renee had not launched her magazine yet, she was still causing a buzz in the backrooms and boardrooms along publisher's row.

"Let's get a drink," Carter said. *I think I'm going to need one.*

The three of them headed toward one of the bars, but his dad was stopped halfway by a guest and his mother paused to greet one of her fashion models, Melanie Esterbrook. Carter continued walking. He didn't want to get caught up with his mother introducing someone beautiful, thin and unmarried. Carter already knew Melanie, but that wouldn't keep his mother from reintroducing them and beginning her sales pitch on the woman's attributes. Not that he wouldn't hear it later in private, but it was much easier to fend off if Melanie wasn't standing in front of him.

The bartender was as much a regular at these parties as his parents. He knew exactly what Carter preferred and reached for a glass when he saw him coming.

The bartender smiled, poured a finger of scotch in a glass, added water and handed it to Carter.

Moving away from the bar, Carter circled the room, talking to the guests, but always aware of the door and that Renee had yet to appear.

"How's it going?" someone from behind him asked.

Carter turned to see another one of his mother's models. She must've been new since Carter didn't recognize her. But then, the faces of models sometimes merged together. He'd been around beautiful women all his life and he supposed he'd built an internal immunity to them and the admiration they expected.

"JoAnna Snow," she said, and offered her hand. She wore a one-shoulder chiffon gown that showed off her creamy skin. She'd pulled her hair to the side, and she looked like she was ready for a photo shoot.

"Carter Hampshire," he said, taking her hand.

"I know." Her voice had just the right amount of sultriness to it.

He knew what was coming, but he smiled and decided to try and sidetrack her request to be on the cover of one of his magazines. "Snow? Is that a real last name or a model identity?"

"It's real. And I'm not a model."

Carter's brows rose. "Most of the people here are either in the fashion business or publishing. Where do you fit?"

"Fit?" She said it as if it was a dirty word. "I hope I'm not being put into a box."

"I apologize. My word choice was poor. It's that my parents usually invite people within the same industry to their parties."

"Apology accepted," she said with a winning smile. "I'm with The Women's Project. We're a nonprofit group that helps women restart their lives."

Carter nodded. It was a noble career.

"Your mother has been very influential in getting donors for us."

Carter glanced across the room at his mother. "She's like that."

JoAnna nodded.

"Did she by any chance tell you that Hampshire Publications would donate to your cause?"

"She did." JoAnna smiled.

"Did she also give you the amount of our donation?"

JoAnna shook her head. Her curls bounced. Carter thought of how Renee's hair bounced when she walked.

"Why don't you call me on Monday, and we'll work something out?" He could see his mother smiling from across the room. She probably knew exactly what had just transpired between them. "In the meantime, would you like to dance?"

That would satisfy his mother, seeing the two of them together. They stepped to the dance floor and circled it a couple of times before Carter saw Renee enter the room. A man came up behind Renee and placed his hands on her arms. The gesture was intimate. Losing his focus, he stepped on JoAnna's foot.

Carter hadn't realized he'd stopped moving and now just stood staring at Renee.

What a reception, Renee thought. She

looked around the huge house — it was brightly lit and filled with people. Renee had been surprised the Hampshires still included her among their guests. But when the invitation had arrived, she couldn't refuse it. And she couldn't go alone. She needed to convince Carter that there was nothing and there would be nothing between them. But there was no one she could ask to escort her who wouldn't read more into it than was there. So she called the only person she knew would fill the bill: her twin brother, Roger.

Renee knew where the bar was, and taking Roger's hand, she headed that way. The bartender recognized her.

"Sweet white wine?" he asked.

Renee smiled. "You remembered."

He nodded, but the smile on his face said more. Roger's presence probably stopped him from the flirting that she knew would have come. From the other room, the band started to play "Night and Day." Carter stood in the doorway, his arms wrapped around a tall woman with dark hair.

Had Carter asked the band to play that song? She wasn't sure how to read his expression. Roger took her elbow and she snapped out of her trance. They walked toward a group of people Renee knew, although she was unsure if she'd be capable of coherent speech.

"Night and Day" had played over and over on the first night they'd spent in bed. Renee had it on a CD and somehow she'd hit the repeat button. Images of them in bed accosted her. She slipped her arm through Roger's and held on tightly.

"You all right?" he whispered.

Releasing her viselike hold on him, she looked up and nodded. For that night, Renee wasn't going to tell anyone Roger was her brother. She'd only introduced him as a biomedical investor, which was technically the truth. Roger did invest in biomedical research. He was the researcher and had his own business that was supported by venture capitalists. Biomedical research was about as far from publishing and fashion as you could get, but he enjoyed explaining it to whomever asked for more information.

"Maybe I'll get some donations from this," he told Renee as they walked into the ballroom and began greeting people. Most of the conversation centered around Roger, since he was the only one there not part of the trade.

Renee's mind was on Carter and the woman he was dancing with. Renee didn't recognize her, but why would she? She was

Carter's date. Renee was silently thankful her brother had agreed to escort her.

As they circled the ballroom, Carter suddenly appeared in front of them. Renee was forced to introduce him. The urge to blurt out the truth was on the tip of her tongue, but Roger interrupted her and offered his hand.

"Nice to meet you," Carter said. "I hope you're enjoying yourself."

"So far it's been good," Roger stated.

Carter checked over his shoulder. "Mind if I ask Renee to dance?"

Roger shook his head and Carter took her hand, giving her no chance to refuse.

"Who is he?" Carter asked, shuttling her around the room.

"My date," she answered. "Someone you don't know."

"Where did you meet him?"

"I think that would fall under the heading of none of your business," Renee said. She had a smile on her face. No one looking at them could have gauged the tension that wrapped around them like shrink-wrap. "Who was the long-haired woman who captured your fancy?"

Renee saw him frown a moment as if he didn't remember the woman. "That was one of my mother's charity directors."

"And you're the charity?" Renee asked, regretting her words the moment they came out. "I'm sorry. I didn't mean to say that."

She stopped dancing, and Carter bumped into her. "I am not the charity, but I will be donating to her cause."

Realizing they were standing in the middle of the dance floor, Renee stepped back. Another couple bumped into them. The music ended and she excused herself. She wove through the crowd looking for her brother. He was nowhere in sight. Forcing herself to walk slowly, she went to the bar and ordered another glass of wine. She moved through the crowd and ended up in a quiet room where many of the current Hampshire magazines were lying on the tables. Renee was naturally drawn to the bridal ones, of which there were three issues.

"Fantastic, aren't they?" a man said near her.

Renee looked at him. She recognized the photographer, but she couldn't remember his name. He'd joined the company just as she was leaving.

"The cover is mine, but the layout inside is a work of art. Are you one of the models?"

Renee shook her head as she opened the magazine and found something she had done in the past.

"I tell you, the last three issues of *Hampshire Bridal* have really rocked," the photographer said.

Renee looked closely and saw that all three issues had used her interior layouts. The gowns inside were new, but everything else had simply been slipped into an existing template she had originally created. She tried to act as if it didn't matter to her, but in fact it did. She was surprised that Carter was allowing this to happen.

"They're not really that new," she said.

"I know. I mean, nothing is really 'new.' " He used both hands to symbolize quote marks. "But the way these have been laid out, the entire flow is stunning."

Renee took her wine glass and excused herself. She passed Carter's father on her way out, and he stopped her.

"Renee, how nice to see you."

He caught her in a bear hug. Joseph Carter had always been friendly. His smile was wide and genuine. Renee liked him.

"I heard you were back at the magazine," he said. "I know it'll be back on top with you in charge."

For a moment, Renee was unsure what magazine he was talking about. "You mean *Hampshire Bridal*? No, I'm not back there."

Joseph Hampshire looked confused. "Then where are you?"

"I'm starting my own magazine."

"You are?"

She nodded.

"Don't you want to head up our division?"

Thankfully, she was saved from answering. Joseph was abruptly pulled away into another conversation.

She stared after him. She'd met Joe Hampshire a few times, mainly at parties and trade events. He was a joker, but always happy. Renee assumed it was his marriage that made him seem as if he walked on clouds. She smiled, hoping one day she'd have someone that made her that happy.

Turning around, she found Roger talking to Carter and her heart stopped. Before she got close to them, they shook hands and Carter left.

"What was that about?" she asked as she joined Roger.

"He was just asking some questions about investing."

"Really?"

"He could have been testing me to see if I knew my stuff, or he could be genuine."

"What did you think?"

"Genuine," Roger said.

Renee felt good about that. She wouldn't

want to find out that Carter had been inter-rogating her brother. But why should she care? Carter was nothing to her. So why had seeing the tall woman in his arms bothered her? The thought came unexpectedly. And why had she felt like Cinderella dancing in his arms?

"Are you ready to go?"

Roger's head turned too quickly. "I'm enjoying this."

"As you are enjoying following that woman in the green dress around."

"You noticed that?"

"Roger, I'm your twin. I just know."

"Well, don't get lost." She leaned close to him and whispered in his ear. "And don't blow my cover."

After-parties were usually laugh-fests. That's what they had been when Carter was in col-lege. He thought of all the nights he and his friends had stumbled out of bed and relived the antics of the night before. After his parents' party, he and his dad had talked most of the night, but no part of their conversation had been humorous.

His mind, as his conversation had been, were about Renee. Carter wondered what she'd done for the rest of the weekend. And he couldn't forget the man she'd been with.

Carter had gone to the party stag. Yet she'd come with a date. It was foolish of him to think that there was no man in her life. Renee was a beautiful woman and he hadn't seen her in three years. It was natural that she'd moved on. Hadn't that been exactly what he wanted her to do? What he'd told her to do when he left?

So why did he feel like there was a hole in his heart? Even when he was away, the one thing he thought leaving her behind would do, hadn't happened. He didn't realize how much he would miss her, how much of her he'd taken with him when he went to Afghanistan. The universe was funny. While Carter thought he was saving both of them, the universe didn't allow it. He'd taken all his feelings and more with him when he'd boarded that plane.

While he was away, he wondered where she was and what she was doing. He wanted to know whom she was with and did she still use the same shampoo. He wanted to know if her hands were still as soft as they were when he held them and if the smile she'd always given him was now being given to someone else.

Carter had his answer. He saw it Friday night in the way she danced with the man whose arm she held. He saw it in the easy manner that the two of them communicated. They almost looked like two halves of the same whole. Had they ever looked like that when they were a couple? Had their communications been that easy?

"You're awfully quiet," Carter's father said. Sitting in the passenger seat, Carter looked out on the scenery between his parents' home and the train station.

"It's getting close to Monday. I was thinking about the office."

His father's laugh was one that said he didn't believe his son for a moment. "Carter, I remember the first time you lost your heart to a girl. You were thirteen. At thirty it's no different. Why don't you tell her how you feel?"

"She's not ready to listen yet. Maybe she will be soon, but right now she still sees me as the man who left her behind. I'm taking it slow. I don't want to push her."

Joe Hampshire parked the car and they got out. Carter reached in the back and pulled his overnight bag out.

"Good advice," Joe said. "Just remember, there are other men out there who might also have an eye for Renee."

Carter nodded. The image of Renee hanging on the arm of the man she was with at the party had him suddenly ready for battle.

"I'll remember."

"I hope so," Carter's father said. "Because I believe your first test is about to happen."

"What?"

His father hitched his chin toward something behind him. Carter turned and looked. Tension tightened his body at what his father meant. Renee stood next to a stairway with the same man she'd been with at the party. She laughed at something he said. Then he hugged her and kissed her cheek. Turning, she bounded up the steps, almost as if she had added buoyancy to her step.

Carter thought she had gone back to New York Friday night. Yet here she was, still on the Island and still with the same man she'd been with at the party. Carter opened his free hand that he'd balled into a fist before loosening his grip on the overnight bag. He hadn't realized he was holding it so tight.

His father's laugh broke into his thoughts. "Have a good trip back. It's bound to be interesting. I'd sure like to be a fly on the wall during your trip."

"I won't even be in the same car with her," Carter said. "She won't know I'm even on the train."

"Yeah, I believe you," his father said, shaking Carter's hand and pulling him into a man-hug. Carter could hear his dad's strong laugh as he backed away and returned to the car.

Turning around to the stairway, Carter scanned the area, looking at as much of the platform that was visible. Renee was no longer in sight. Carter couldn't decide whether or not that was a good thing. For his peace of mind, it was better that he kept some distance between them.

But could he?

Did he want to?

Carter heard the train coming and headed for the platform. When he came out to see his parents and took the train, he usually sat near the end of the train. There were less people there and he could get some work done. Stepping through the door in his usual place, he put his bag in the over-head rack and took his usual seat. He wasn't going to go car by car and find where Renee was sitting.

Ten minutes later the train pulled out of the station. Carter's laptop lay unopened on his knees. Staring out of the window, he watched the platform end and rooftops begin to slide by. The train picked up speed while he thought of Renee sitting ahead of him a few train cars away. Another ten more minutes passed and he opened the laptop and looked at the blank screen. However, he hadn't done much more.

Making a snap decision, he closed the laptop and stood up. Grabbing his bag from the overhead rack, he walked determinately to the car door. Pulling it open, he ignored the Do Not Cross Between Cars While Train is in Motion sign and stepped across the gap. She wasn't in the next car. Carter kept moving. As he opened the doors, all heads were facing front. He would have to identify Renee from the back.

Five cars up, he saw her. The morning sun beamed through her dark brown hair adding halos of red highlights. He could have picked her out no matter which direction she faced. The seat next to her was empty. He walked directly to it, tossed his bag on the rack next to hers and dropped into the seat.

She glanced at him, then did a double take. The book on her lap fell to the floor. Both of them reached for it. Their hands met and Renee quickly pulled hers free.

"Carter!" she said.

"Have a nice weekend?" he asked.

For a long moment, Renee said nothing. She was obviously too surprised at seeing him to speak.

"With all the seats on this train, why do

you want this one?"

"Time goes by faster when you're with a friend," he answered, and offered her the book.

"Friend? We're not friends."

"Of course we are. You don't want to toss people out like Kleenex. You'll find yourself alone in the world."

"Maybe I'd prefer that."

"Believe me, you wouldn't. So, did you have a nice weekend? I thought you went back to the city Friday night, but I see you had company."

"Do you really want to say that and leave yourself open for the obvious reply?"

"That you didn't go back Friday?" he asked.

"That there are a lot of things you don't know about me?"

"We can fix that," he said.

"We can't," Renee contradicted. "But for the record, I had a wonderful weekend. Your parents were gracious to invite me. They've always been very nice to me, especially when your father still ran the business."

Carter felt the obvious barb she'd thrown. "He speaks well of you. In fact, he wondered if you were back at Hampshire Publications."

"Does he still come into the office once in

a while?" Renee asked.

"He says he doesn't want to step on my toes. And that he enjoys sitting by the ocean and letting other people do the work."

"I doubt that. He was always so active."

"He still is. He got a job at the local newspaper, one of the free ones, and writes a weekly column on business. And he's taken up tennis and golf."

"Exercise is probably good for him."

Carter nodded. "His doctor suggested he get into a routine."

"What about you? Are you still swimming?"

"I got some laps in while I was there. I go to the fitness club several times a week and swim." Carter had been on the swim team in college and he still enjoyed the pool.

"What about you, after the party? Did you get in any exercise?" He hated the way that sounded.

Renee smiled. "I did," she said. "In fact, I got a lot in."

"With . . ." He stopped the question. "What did you do?"

"We ran along the beach"

"We?" he interrupted.

"Roger and I, the man who came to the party with me."

Carter nodded. "Does he live on the Island?"

"He has a house there. It was very relaxing to spend the weekend by the sea. I hope to do it more often."

"Did Roger invite you back?" Carter hated the way he talked about the man she'd been seeing. He wanted to know about him, but then he didn't.

"Roger is a biomedical researcher. I'm considering investing in his business."

"That could be very risky. You could lose your entire investment."

"I know, but Roger would take care of me," Renee said. She tossed her head and pushed her hair away from her face. It was curly and Carter wanted to run his hands through it. He knew it was thick and silky and he could get just as much tangled in it as he could in her. He wondered what she meant by Roger would take care of her. Was he doing that now? Did she need someone to take care of her? Why hadn't she turned to him?

Carter knew why. He knew that he'd left her almost standing at the altar. They weren't engaged. They hadn't gotten that far, at least not with spoken words, but they knew they'd crossed the line. And that was when Carter had decided to end things. He was leaving and he didn't want any entanglements behind. He never expected to feel so strongly for Renee, especially when he knew he would be gone in weeks.

But the fire between them flared, then raged out of control. Telling her he didn't want to see her anymore was the hardest thing he'd ever had to say. Now seeing her, being within reach of her and not being able to say what he wanted, to touch her, hold her, make love to her was tearing him apart.

The train reached Penn Station in New York faster than he thought possible. Passengers got to their feet, preparing to disembark. How could he keep Renee from leaving? He didn't want to part from her. He wanted to stay near her, even if he couldn't touch or hold her. He still wanted her around.

"Do you have a car waiting?" Carter asked.

"I'm taking a taxi," she said. "I only have a small bag. Everything else I left at Roger's."

The mention of the man's name pierced him as surely as a switchblade knife would have. What kind of relationship did she have with him? Carter swallowed his retort on what he thought of Roger.

They exited the train together. Throngs of

people spilled out of the train and headed in all directions. Some scrambled to make connections. Others headed for the New York Subway System. Some rushed outside to catch an available taxi. Carter focused on keeping up with Renee.

"Here, let me take that for you." Carter took her backpack before she could refuse. She couldn't ditch him if he had her makeup and jewelry. He was sure that's what she carried. He wasn't sure that green gown she'd worn was inside, but whatever was there was valuable to her and she'd want it back.

Renee looked at him suspiciously, but allowed him to keep the bag.

"How do you find being back in a place where people are always moving? Tourists never stop coming, no matter the weather and there are crowds everywhere. I guess it's a lot different from the streets of Princeton, NJ."

"Every city is different," Renee said. "I like New York with all the things you mentioned. I also have a house in Princeton that I kept. So if the crowds, tourists and anyone else . . ." she glanced at him when she said that ". . . gets in my way, I have a sanctuary."

"Do you think you need a sanctuary?"

"You never know. After all, this is a very big city. I might need some place to relax."

They reached the escalator leading up to Seventh Avenue. A car was waiting by the curb. Carter went straight for it. He opened the door and stood back for her to get in. Renee looked at the taxi stand and the long line of people waiting.

"I'll take you wherever you need to go," Carter said.

"It's out of your way. I'll take my backpack and be gone."

She reached for it. Her hand touched the strap and Carter turned to face her. Someone bumped into them, pushing them closer together.

"You're not so scared of being alone with me that you can't accept the offer of a ride, are you?"

"Of course I'm not afraid of you. I wonder that you want to be in the area with me."

She stepped around him and slid into the back seat. Carter knew she had no idea how much he wanted to be in the same place with her.

Renee gave him her address and the driver pulled away from the curb. As much as she chided Carter, she was nervous of him. Her body was hot and she could feel a stream of sweat rolling between her breasts. The car was air conditioned, but it couldn't keep up with her personal furnace. The drive was amazingly short.

The driver opened the door and Renee slid out without answering his question. Carter came out behind her.

"I'm all right, Carter. There's no need for you to come. The door is barely ten feet away and it's broad daylight."

"It would insult my mother's teachings if I didn't see you safely inside."

Renee looked up at him. He was clearly the most handsome man she'd ever seen. "Does that mean you need to check every room inside to make sure no terrorists or ninjas have eluded my alarm system in the last three days?"

"Only if you think it's necessary."

CHAPTER 5

Wanda and Pete arrived in the bridal department at the same time the next morning.

Renee looked at Pete with concern. "You look like you didn't sleep at all last night," she said.

"I didn't," he said.

"Why not?" Wanda ask. "We don't launch for a while. If you can't sleep now, by the time we get there, you'll be a nervous wreck."

"I'm already a wreck. Did you pick up a magazine on your way in today?" Pete asked Renee.

She shook her head. She usually did. She knew exactly when the new magazines hit the newsstands. And she was often there to get a first copy. Today, she'd been a little preoccupied. It wasn't that she didn't sleep well. She'd hadn't been thinking about the magazine. Carter was on her mind.

Pete lifted a copy of the current issue of

Hampshire Bridal he was holding and slid it across the desk. Renee picked it up.

"Beautiful isn't it?"

She gasped at the cover. Coming forward in her chair, she pulled the magazine closer. Opening it, she leafed through the pages. Color drained from her face.

"I know," Wanda said. "It's gorgeous. I had the same reaction."

Renee's reaction was different. She recognized a lot about it. It was different in some places, but for the most part, Renee was familiar with the layout. Why was it here? There were only so many ways to put people on a page, and Hampshire did own this layout. There was no reason they couldn't use it. Renee was just surprised to see it.

By the time she left work that night, she was still thinking about *Hampshire Bridal.* Going to a newsstand, she panned the array of copies like the one she was taking home with her. Laying it on the coffee table in her living room, she found it staring at her each time she passed. She had to find the truth. When she'd moved to Princeton, she'd put a lot of her things in storage. She had yet to get them out and unpack them. She couldn't get a physical copy or a previous magazine, but she might be able to find the CD where she'd saved the files.

It took her two hours to find it in one of the boxes that was still unpacked and sitting in her would-be home office as soon as she had time to organize it. The files were over three years old and the program that had created them had been updated several times since. She hoped it would open.

Renee put the CD in the disc drive and waited. Finally it opened and she watched the screen. Looking back and forth between the computer and the book on her desk, she saw the similarity. More than similarity. If there was such a thing as plagiarizing a previous issue, Hampshire had done it. And done it with a past layout that she had designed.

Sighing, Renee knew there was nothing she could say or do about it. She'd been employed at Hampshire when she created it. And it belonged to them to do with what they wished. But why were they recycling a previous spread? And why were they making it so obvious that they had done little to disguise it.

The next time she saw Blair, she would ask. Then Renee thought better of it. It was none of her business. If Hampshire wanted to use a previous design and layout, they had every right. And he might think she was trying to take credit for it. It was better to leave it alone. She had *Designed for Brides* to worry about and there was enough going on there to keep her busy until the launch. She didn't need to get sidetracked by a misinterpretation with Hampshire.

After a moment, a smile stole across Renee's face. They were afraid, she thought. She could hear her own voice as a whisper in her mind. They were afraid of her. The smile widened. Renee lifted the glossy book and looked at it. She could tell their fear had translated into imitation. They couldn't stop her, couldn't even discover what she was doing to launch her project, so they were going to match her using her own designs. Suddenly, Renee's energy level soared as if she'd had a drug infusion.

Fear was a powerful motivator. Renee saw it in the pages of *Hampshire Bridal.* And Hampshire had reason to fear. They just didn't know how much.

But they would find out and soon.

Not having to go into the office, even for a single day, made Renee feel less claustrophobic. A shipment of dresses for a scheduled photo shoot was expected, and since the office was being painted and set up, there was no place to store them. Renee had moved into her own space, so she'd had them sent to the guesthouse. Dana had come to the city for the weekend to visit, and Renee enlisted her to help with opening boxes and hanging gowns.

"Oh, this is gorgeous," Dana said as she pulled a gown from a box.

She'd said the same thing for each box she opened and each gown she hung. Renee laughed. Dana's comment took her back to her consulting days. They weren't that far behind her, yet hearing a bride find the perfect dress for her special day still gave her goose bumps.

"Renee, you have got to let me try some of these on."

"I take it you're not superstitious," Renee said sarcastically.

"Not in the least." Dana held up a dress covered in Battenburg lace. The sigh she gave was audible and appreciative. "Teddy should do this all the time."

"It is taking more and more of her time. I wouldn't be surprised if sooner or later, she and Diana hire someone else to do the consulting while Teddy concentrates full-time on design."

"And with the magazine you're doing showcasing these dresses, she'll be busier than ever."

"That's the plan," Renee said and smiled.

They had ten boxes to unpack. Seven contained gowns and the other three held accessories.

"When is the shoot?" Dana asked. "I want to be here for that."

"It's on Monday. Can you stay over? I could use the help."

Dana looked at her as if she'd been granted access to Fort Knox.

"I can stay," she said quickly. "That is, unless you have plans." Her brows went up. "Like, is that hunk Carter coming over?"

"Dana," Renee warned. She kept her head down, looking at the task she was performing. "I've told you more than once that Carter and I are history. We never really had a history, so even that may be a misnomer."

"You have and I've heard you, but I'm not convinced that all is done."

"All is done. You sound like someone out of the eighteenth century.

"It must be the gown." Dana held up a retro dress made of delicate lace and covered in pearls. "I think I'll die if you don't let me try this on."

The gown was definitely a magazine cover. She wondered which model was destined to wear it for the shoot on Monday. But for the moment, her cousin would be the first.

"Do you think it will fit?" Renee asked.

"I don't know. It doesn't have a size." Dana looked for a tag. "And models are usually super thin."

"Let's try it."

Moments later, Renee was holding the dress and slipping it over Dana's head. Delicately, she helped Dana pull the gown down and Renee meticulously buttoned her into it.

"Oh," Dana said, looking down at herself.

"You are going to be a beautiful bride," Renee told her cousin. Renee pulled a full-length mirror designated for the shoot in front of Dana. "Look," she said.

Dana's hand went to her breasts. "Is that me?"

"See what a great gown can do for a bride?"

Dana twisted from side to side, looking at herself.

"Let me get the veil and gloves."

"And my phone so I can take a picture," Dana called. "It's in my purse."

The gown could have been made for Dana. The train was long and Renee pulled it out, unfolding the lace and spreading it behind her cousin almost to the length of the room. Renee found a veil and stood on the sofa to set it on her cousin's head.

"Oh," she sighed when she jumped down

and looked at Dana. "Oh, my," she whispered, awed by the way her cousin looked. "It's you."

Standing back, Renee snapped a photo on her phone.

"Take one on my phone," Dana said. "I want to show it to my mom."

Renee laughed and took several pictures. "Be careful with that. You know what will happen. You'll have to explain to your mom why you were trying on wedding gowns."

"It's only *one* gown."

"She'll overlook that point," Renee laughed, thinking of her aunt. "She'll want to know who the guy is, why she hasn't met him and whether there's a date yet."

Renee continued to click the shutter. Dana turned about as if she was truly modeling the gown.

"All right. Give me a happy pose. One that you'd find on the cover of a romance novel."

Dana laughed. She pulled the veil off and held it in her hand while it dragged on the floor. Then she threw her head back and arched her back.

"Perfect." Renee was having fun. "Send these to me, especially that last one."

Dana took the phone and pressed several buttons.

"They're in your email. Now you."

"I could never look like you in that dress."

"Not this one. I saw you looking long and hard at one of Teddy's originals. Come on, I tried one on. You can do the same."

"All right," Renee said. She helped Dana take the dress off, then went to the collection they'd hung on the makeshift rack. Sorting through them, she found the one she loved. The strapless bodice was covered in Swarovski crystals shaped like flowers. Between them other crystals dripped like falling teardrops. The bottom of the gown was two layers of white satin over a huge underskirt. The bodice was covered in lace appliqués that picked up the crystals. The train wasn't as long as the one Dana had worn, but it spread out in a perfect semicircle.

Dana found fingerless gloves that reached Renee's elbows and again sported the dripping crystals. While Renee pulled them on, Dana placed the matching veil over Renee's hair.

"Wow," she said stepping back. "You should be one of the models. You look . . ." Dana stopped.

"Dana, are you crying?"

"Of course I'm not crying . . ." Her voice broke. "Where's my phone?" Covering her tears, Dana found the cell phone and took several photos. "Turn around," she said. "I want some with the train twisted."

Doing as Dana said, Renee turned a step. Dana pushed the mirror around and Renee got a glimpse of herself. She gasped at the reflection. For a moment she couldn't speak.

"Stand over here," Dana instructed.

Renee moved. The dress and all its slips were heavy. Renee went up two steps and turned back.

"Right there," Dana raised a hand and Renee stopped. "Don't fix anything. It's perfect."

The camera clicked as Dana took one shot after another. "Take some with my phone," Renee said.

"I want a romance cover pose, too," Dana said.

"Fine, but I need a romance cover hero."

"I suppose you'll have to pretend Carter is holding you."

Renee stood up straight and stared directly at Dana. "You think Carter is cover model material?"

She nodded. "Go ahead, lie to me. Tell me you don't think Carter Hampshire could compete with any of those shirtless, airbrushed men on the books you read."

"All right, I concede. He'd a good-looking man."

"He's a great-looking man. I'm sure women are falling all over themselves to get to him."

"Do you mind if we don't talk about Carter?"

Dana hunched her shoulders and snapped another photo.

"Enough," Renee said. "If we're going to make that play tonight, we need to finish this."

Renee came down the steps and turned so Dana could unzip the gown.

"Just a minute. I want to send some of these to myself. I can't be the only one my mother sees in a wedding gown. Where are your contacts? Never mind — I see them."

Setting the phone on the coffee table, she unzipped the gown and held it as Renee stepped out of it.

Renee took the dress and delicately replaced it on the padded hanger. Then she slipped it back into its plastic bag and went to the dress rack. Why did Dana have to bring up Carter? Now all Renee could think about was him holding her in that romance cover pose. As soon as Dana had said it, Renee had gone all warm inside, as if she could feel his strong hands holding her. Suddenly she wished they were holding her.

■ ■ ■ ■

The pool water was refreshing. Carter swam his thirtieth lap, then pulled himself out of the water and grabbed a plush towel. Drying himself, he breathed hard as he flopped down on a nearby chaise lounge on the fitness center's roof swimming deck. He could feel the sun through the overhead glass panels. It was warm and Carter relaxed for several minutes. A single note that pinged on his cell phone told him he had a new message. Usually he turned the sound off on weekends and late at night. Since he was expecting a call from his sister and she was partial to texting, he'd left it on. The ping, however, wasn't a text. It was an email.

And it was from Renee.

He sat up straight, staring at the phone. Seeing her name and her photo was so unexpected Carter nearly dropped the phone. Leaning forward, his legs balanced on both sides of the chair, he opened the message. There were no comments, only several attached image files. Why would Renee send him picture files? And why was there no message accompanying them?

Carter checked the address. It was hers and there were no other addresses in the email indicating that it could be spam mail or a virus. Curiosity got the best of him and he clicked on the first file. It took a moment, but a photo of Renee appeared wearing a wedding gown. All the air seemed to leave his lungs when he saw her. She was as beautiful as any of the models he'd seen in the magazines.

What did this mean, he asked himself.

He opened the second file. Again, it was Renee. She wore the same dress, but her position and pose were different. Carter had the same reaction. Not only did his breath stop, his heart hammered. What was going on? Renee had rebuffed him at every turn, then out of the blue she sends him wedding photos as if she was part of the upcoming spread in a Hampshire bridal magazine.

There had to be a reason. Renee was a straight forward person. She'd told him in no uncertain terms that she wanted nothing to do with him. So what the heck was this?

Carter opened the third file. Renee's eyes were dreamy. She had the look a photographer would give anything to capture — the look of love. Staring directly at him, love poured from Renee's eyes, showing whoever she was looking at or thinking about that she loved him. Carter was sure it was a *him.* Should he read anything into these photos?

He was too confused. Why had she sent them? And without a message. What was she trying to tell him?

He had to know.

His calls to Renee had been unanswered and unreturned. However, Blair told him she had a photo shoot Monday morning. *Well models weren't the only thing she was going to see that day,* he thought.

CHAPTER 6

Monday came way too soon. Renee and Dana had relived the old days, when they were carefree and only interested in talking their dads into buying them new dresses for the school dance. They'd spent a night at a play, then followed it up with drinks at a local bar, which turned into a dance marathon. Recuperation on Sunday would have been ideal, except that Renee had to make sure all the details were set and ready for the shoot early Monday morning.

And it wouldn't be just morning. They had to be ready before sunrise, while the mist was still in the air. They were beginning in a park north of the city. But the photographers had other places they wanted to photograph the models, including a ruined mansion. Thankfully, all the models were there on time. Renee had sent cars to pick them up to make sure. It was going to be a long day.

"All right people, let's do this," the photographer shouted. The first group of models came out of the temporary dressing room, each holding her dress and train to keep them clean.

Dana sidled up to Renee. "Excited?" Renee asked. "Have you ever been to a shoot before?"

Dana shook he head. "This is fascinating. I wish I could model that gown I fell in love with."

"You've got the pictures," Renee told her.

Dana pulled her phone out as a model emerged wearing the dress. Both women looked at the phone and then at the model in front of them.

"That is one gorgeous dress," Dana said. "And she's wearing it to death."

"She doesn't look any better in it than you did," Renee chided with a smile.

"She's had a hairstylist and a makeup artist work on her, plus she's tall as the Empire State Building."

"But how did you feel in the dress?"

"Like it was *my* day."

"Wait, here comes your dress. Let me pull up the photo." The two of them watched as image after image of Renee flashed by. Dana frowned and started the sequence over.

"What's wrong?" Renee asked.

"Some of them are missing." She went through her photos again. Renee peered from next to her.

"Where's the romance one?" Renee asked.

"You sent it to yourself. It should be in your email."

"Right," Dana said and pulled up her email. Renee saw her name in the unopened messages. Dana opened the file and clicked on the photos. The two of them looked as Dana smiled for the camera and her cousin. "Wait, these are the ones of me. I opened the wrong file."

She went back to the inbox. There was no other message from Renee.

"They're on my phone." Renee pulled her phone from the pocket of her jeans and opened her email. "Here they are." Again the two of them looked at the photos and at the model wearing the gown.

"Wait a minute," Dana said. "Why don't I have those on my phone, too?"

"Check your sent folder," Dana said. "Maybe the files are still in your outbox waiting to process."

Renee opened her sent folder and froze. There was the email Dana had sent from Renee's phone. But it wasn't addressed to Dana. It was addressed to Carter.

"Oh, no!" Renee wailed. Everyone in the

yard turned to look at her.

"What's wrong?" Dana asked.

Renee could barely speak. "You didn't send those pictures to yourself."

"I did," Dana defended. "You were standing there when I sent the message.

"Look." Renee held up her phone and pointed to the message in her sent folder.

Dana gasped. "I couldn't have done that."

Renee understood what had happened. Carter was in her address book and Dana had had a hard time finding the contact list. When she'd pressed the small key for her contact information, she'd probably hit Carter's instead.

"I'm so sorry, Renee. I never intended to send those photos to him."

Renee didn't say anything. She nodded to her cousin. As much as Dana teased her, she would never have sent those photos without Renee's knowledge.

"What are we going to do now?" Dana asked.

"It's my problem," Renee said.

"I can explain it to him," Dana said. "It was my mistake. I can fix it."

"You can't," Renee said quietly. She took Dana's arm and squeezed it, letting her know she understood it was an error. Renee should have removed his number from her contact list years ago. But she hadn't.

Suddenly, Dana grabbed Renee's arm and squeezed it so tight it hurt. Renee cried out in pain and Dana loosened her grip, but did not release her. "Don't look around," she whispered.

"Why?"

"He's over there. Behind you."

Fear raced through Renee, cold and heavy. "Who?"

"Carter Hampshire."

Renee was tired. Strain from finding Carter staring at her and her need to direct the shoot warred in her mind and body. Life had been a whirlwind for the past three weeks and it culminated with her needing to explain the misdirected photos.

"Let me go tell him what happened," Dana said for the second time.

Renee shook her head. "I'll do it."

Giving Dana a quick smile, she turned and went toward Carter. His face held the slight reflection of a smirk. She wondered if he knew how uncomfortable she felt.

"Great photo," he said the moment she was within earshot.

"I can explain that."

"Don't. I'd rather imagine it. I wish I could have been there," he teased.

"Carter, I need you to delete those pictures."

He crossed his arms and planted his feet. "Now why would I do that?"

Renee knew only the truth would do. "The gown I wore is the centerpiece of our first issue. I need to make sure it's not unveiled until the launch."

Carter looked at the sky as if he was thinking.

"I know you won't use the dress to embarrass me." She appealed to his sense of honor.

He slipped his phone from his pocket and punched in his security code.

Renee held her breath, hoping his intent was to comply with her wishes.

"Is this the one?" He turned the phone so she could see the display.

Renee nodded, although she was sure Carter knew that was the one. Dana had only sent one message to his address.

Going back to the message, he clicked the file to select it. His finger hovered over the delete key. Before pressing it he looked at her.

"What do I get for doing this?"

Renee stepped back as if the question pushed her. "You want to negotiate for the photos?"

"Seems like a good time to me." His smile was white and irritating.

Vowing to remain calm, she asked, "What do you want?"

He stepped closer to her and leaned in. Renee felt the heat of his skin.

"I get the photo back after the launch."

Relief spread through her. Renee's mind had gone in an entirely different direction.

"Is that all?" she asked.

"All for now."

Carter smiled at the mocked-up layout on his desk. "Blair, these are fantastic. Did you hire someone I don't know to design these?"

Blair was shaking her head. Her smile was huge. Carter supposed he'd been harsh with her when he'd rejected the campaign she'd brought to him previously. She had to be relieved that he now liked what she'd presented.

"It was hard to take, but you know when we have to come up with something fantastic, we stand up to the challenge."

"And that you did," Carter said. "You should have been doing these all along. I think they can compete with anything out there. Not only compete, but surpass."

"Thanks," Blair said. "I have more on the

drawing board if you'd like to see them now."

"These six are fine. You have my approval," Carter said. "Go with them. We'll have to check out some of the designer collections and get the results of the photo shoots. But I have to say, I am impressed."

Blair gathered the layouts. "We've been working hard in the department."

"Well, please thank everyone for the work. Usually these designs take months. You've done them in just a few weeks."

"And I'm exhausted," she said. "It was a gargantuan effort. Thankfully, we don't have to continue at that level. We've got six months of layouts ready to go under our belts. Now we can breathe a while."

Carter nodded. He felt so much better. For some reason he knew *Hampshire Bridal* would compete with whatever Renee was doing. When her first issue launched later this year, he wanted to have something that was comparable, if not better. Blair had come through, but then she knew this business backward and forward. After all, she'd hired Renee and tutored her. Then Renee's talent had taken flight, and the magazine sales had begun surpassing all projections. It hadn't been the same since she'd left, since he'd forced her to resign.

He was happy that she was using her talent again. It was impossible for him to want her to fail.

It was impossible for him not to want her.

"You seem to have found your energy barometer," Wanda said when Renee arrived at the office the next day.

She smiled but offered no answer. She knew it was the plan she had in motion that had caused the change in her.

"Sit down," Renee said. "I want to explain an idea I have. I hope with your design wizardry you can make it a reality."

By the time Renee stepped into the elevator that night, she was walking on air. If the two of them pulled her idea together, the industry would be set on its ear and she'd sell a ton of magazines.

Checking the hallways for any sign of Carter, she began walking toward the exit. Sighing as the fresh air hit her, she felt as if she'd escaped him one more day. Yet she felt a twinge of loss. She didn't want to run into Carter, but when she didn't she felt as something was missing.

Renee turned left out of the building. She lived toward the right, but that's how Carter would head. Ten steps later, she noticed a commotion at the curb. Two men were talking in a panic in front of an open car.

One of them was Carter.

What was happening? Without thinking Renee rushed to him.

"Carter, what's wrong?"

"I have to go." He pulled the car door open. "My dad had a heart attack."

His voice was slightly emotional. Renee put her hand on his arm.

"They don't think he's going to make it."

Renee sucked in a breath. "He's on the island, right?" The Hampshires had moved to the Hamptons when Carter's father retired.

Carter nodded.

"You're not driving?" she questioned.

"No other way to get there. The next train doesn't leave for two hours."

Renee bit her bottom lip. Then, making a snap decision, she took his keys and slid into the driver's seat.

"I'm driving," she said. "Get in."

Carter waited a long second, staring into her eyes. Emotions she was unaware of crowded into her.

"He'll be all right," she said, her voice only a whisper of sound.

Carter shut the door and moved to the passenger seat. Renee pulled into the traffic flow as soon as he'd clicked the seat belt.

Carter was quiet for the ride through the city. Once they got through the Midtown Tunnel, his shoulders relaxed a little.

"The doctor called," he said without her asking. "He said the heart attack was serious and that I should come."

Renee let him talk. Putting her hand on his leg was all the comfort she could give. Carter covered her hand with his, and Renee bit her bottom lip.

They drove straight to the Hampton Regional Medical Center. Carter was out of the car the moment she cut the engine. He didn't wait for her as he headed for the entrance, but Renee was only a step behind him. They found his mother in the hall on the third floor, and Carter went into her arms.

"How is he?" Carter asked.

"He's sleeping." She glanced at a door. Carter followed her glance.

"I'm going in." He took his mother's arms from around him and stepped back. He kissed her on the temple and went through the door.

Renee went to Mrs. Hampshire. The woman looked up at her in confusion, then recognition. "Renee?" she said.

Renee nodded.

"You work for Carter?"

"I used to," she corrected.

Renee draped her arm around the woman. She seemed small and lost. Renee led her to a small room with seats where they sat down. Renee had met Emily Hampshire several times and liked her. She always dressed like a fashion model and wore only her own designs. Today, though, she just looked like a distraught wife unsure of his husband's condition.

"Carter's been in there a long time," she said.

"It's only been a few minutes. He'll be out soon."

She patted Renee's hand. The action was nervous and self-conscious.

"Can I do anything for you?" Renee asked. Emily Hampshire looked like she needed sleep. "I have a car. I can take you home to rest for an hour or so."

"No!" She drew away. "I can't leave."

Renee pulled her back and let her lean against her. "We'll wait."

Carter came in a few minutes later, and Emily popped up like a champagne cork. Her steps took her back to Carter.

"The doctor came in while I was there," he explained. "He's in serious condition. There's no guarantee. The next twenty-four hours will tell."

"Twenty-four hours, then what?"

Carter sighed. Renee knew the answer and knew he didn't want to say the words out loud.

"He'll be fine," Renee said, coming up behind her. "The best thing you can do is go home and rest."

"No," Emily said again.

"You want him to see you at your best. You can rest, eat and come back."

Renee glanced at Carter. He nodded. "I'll stay here," he told his mother. "I'll call if there's any change."

Reluctantly, she nodded. Carter walked them to the door. He hugged his mother, then squeezed Renee's hand.

She looked up at Carter, and they locked eyes.

Carter needed her.

CHAPTER 7

The Hampshire home was a sprawling three-story mansion accented with fish-scale shingles. At the end of the house was a double-story attached gazebo. The back faced the sea, and Renee smelled the water. It was beautiful and breathtaking. During the party, she hadn't been able to see the water, but she knew what the view looked like from other parties she'd attended.

A maid opened the door as soon as Renee stopped the car. Together they took Mrs. Hampshire inside.

"She needs to rest and eat," Renee said.

The maid directed her to the master bedroom and left them to get her a tray.

The inside of the house was just as beautiful as the outside — open, bright and happy looking. Renee had been there before, but never above the ground floor. Together she and Mrs. Hampshire went up a staircase that any five-star hotel would be proud to display. Carter's mother didn't argue about resting, and she was nearly asleep when the maid came in.

After eating half a sandwich and drinking some tea, she refused everything else and fell asleep. Renee took the tray and quietly stole out of the room. As she descended the stairs, she heard a car door slam. Checking the window, she saw a yellow cab and the top of a man's head. A moment later, the front door opened and in walked a man resembling Carter. He was an inch or two shorter, but they had the same dark eyes and smooth skin. Dropping an overnight bag by the door, he looked up at Renee.

"Who are you?" he asked.

"I'm Renee Hart. You must be one of Carter's brothers." She knew he had three brothers and a sister.

"Sean," he said. "Where's my mother?"

Coming to stand in front of him, she said, "She's sleeping. I got her to eat a little. Carter's at the hospital."

"How is he?"

She knew he referred to his father and not Carter.

"The doctor said it's too early to tell. They're hoping to know more by this time tomorrow."

"I'll run up and see my mom, then get my

car and go there."

"Try not to wake her. She's really tired," Renee said.

"Are you a nurse?" he asked.

"No, I'm just a friend." Although right now the lines of what she was seemed to be blurring.

Renee was in the living room looking through the windows at the darkness when Sean came back down.

"I'm on my way out," he said.

She turned. "I'll stay with her until she wakes. Carter promised to call if there was any change."

He started toward the back of the house.

"Sean?"

He stopped.

"Take this." Renee handed him a small insulated pouch. "It's got juice in it for Carter. He's not a big coffee drinker." She didn't add that coffee made him restless. He was probably restless enough.

"You must know him well."

"We used to work together," she offered. "When everyone was drinking coffee, he'd have a bottle of juice."

Sean took the bag from her. "You're Renee, right?"

She nodded, wondering if he'd forgotten her name or if he was remembering it.

"Thanks," he said. But it was his smile, so like Carter's that made her feel that he knew more than he was letting on.

Carter didn't call. Mrs. Hampshire was still asleep when Renee looked in on her two hours later. Renee didn't know her well enough to know if she should wake her or let her rest. She opted to let the woman rest. Neither of her sons had returned to the house, and they would have come or called if there was any news.

At sunrise, a group of people came through the door. Their noise woke Renee, who'd fallen asleep on the sofa. She pushed her hair out of her face.

"How is he?" she asked, pushing her bare feet to the floor.

Carter came to her. "He's out of danger."

Renee stood up and Carter pulled her into his arms. She closed her eyes and held on, relieved about his father, but also loving the feel of being held by him. Loving it too much. She needed to push him back, but found it was too hard.

"Do you think we could get introduced to this woman in your arms?"

The voice came from the only other female in the room. Carter stepped back and turned, his arm remaining possessively around her waist. He introduced her to his other brothers, Sloan and Shane, and his sister Julia. Renee smiled and shook hands with them all.

"It's good news about your father," she said.

"What news?"

All eyes went to the staircase. Mrs. Hampshire was halfway down. Her children moved to her, and only Carter stayed behind.

Renee turned to him. "I have to go back now."

"Don't go."

She so wanted to fall into the darkness of his eyes, but she knew better. "I have things to do. Your father is out of danger. You have your mom and your family for support. I need to go back to work."

Carter sighed, but didn't try to stop her. "I'll drive you to the train station."

Renee nodded and said goodbye to the group. His mother came over and thanked her with a hug.

At the station, Carter got out of the car and waited on the platform with her. It was crowded with the morning's rush hour commuters.

"You don't need to wait. You've been up all night, and you need to get some rest."

"The train will be here soon. And I wanted to thank you for all you did."

"No need." She looked down at the platform.

"You dropped everything you planned for the evening, drove me out here, listened to me in the car, cared for my mother and remembered that I needed juice."

Renee laughed at the last.

Carter smiled.

"Only a friend would do that," he said. "We can't be strangers any longer."

The wind blew against her, but the heat invading her body was no match for it. Looking over her shoulder, she saw the train's engine light in the distance.

"That's my train," she said unnecessarily, but feeling like she needed to say something to keep her emotions in check.

"I'll see you when I get back," he said.

Renee nodded. Carter pulled her into his arms and kissed her. His mouth was hard on hers and Renee's was just as hard on his. Strong arms circled her body, pulling her close, until the train whistled.

"I have to go," she said, her voice hoarse and her emotions raw. Pulling away, she moved onto the train, turning back to look at Carter. The crowd forced her further away from where he stood. She wanted him, needed him. When he'd come through the door at his house, he'd come straight to her and taken her into his arms as if it was the most natural thing to do. As if it was what he should do.

For the merest moment, Renee felt as if she belonged there. As if she was part of that family and they were part of hers.

The next day, Renee woke refreshed and ready to go back to her work plans, which were becoming more concrete by the day.

As long as she lived, she would consider hiring Wanda one of her smartest moves ever. The woman was incredible. The two of them had worked tirelessly for weeks coming up with the computerized program that was the first part of the plan Renee had in mind. Neither had told anyone what they were doing. They were almost ready for the launch party, and Renee planned to invite Diana and Teddy up for the unveiling. They were using one of Teddy's creations, which Renee would model while Wanda would handle the graphics.

The final result came at midnight two weeks after Carter returned to the office. Renee hadn't seen him. But the tension of potentially running into him had a greater force than it had in the past. Renee knew it had to do with the kiss on the platform. With all his kisses.

"It was an absolutely stupendous idea," Wanda said as they looked at the spinning gown.

Her comment pulled Renee's attention back to the present.

"I wish I'd thought of it."

Renee discovered Wanda liked to speak in superlatives. Everything was over the top.

Renee's idea was to use a new technology that would create a hologram of a wedding gown. They had needed a hologram expert, and so Wanda had called in Pete Cooper, who she knew did this kind of work. He was fabulous. Renee had hired him as a consultant, but eventually changed his position to full time employee.

They were about to finalize the last test to make sure the system worked.

"You were so right to patent this," Pete told her as he fiddled with the device on his arm.

"Just wait until the competition finds out what we have. We won't be able to keep these magazines on the newsstands," Wanda said, her fingers flashing over the computer keys like lightning striking.

"I hope Ms. Teddy is ready for the onslaught of brides," Pete said.

"I've already given her a heads-up. They're planning to be ready."

Renee was holding ground-breaking technology. It would bring business in, and not just for the magazine. Teddy had a store in Princeton, but there was no New York facility, not to mention all the places across the United States where the magazine would be available. She needed to call Teddy and set up a meeting. This was a new business and they needed to plan for the operation.

"How close are we to being ready?" Renee asked.

"Just inches," Pete said.

"Call me when we're ready for the test."

"I'd say you should go refresh your makeup. We're that close." Wanda took a moment to glance at her and smile.

Moments later Renee stood in the middle of the floor. Wanda stood on one side of the room, Peter on the other.

"Ready," he asked.

"As ready as ever," she said. Lifting her arm, she pressed the button on the strap Wanda had hooked on her. A mockup of the magazine was propped against the desk, with one of Teddy's gown designs facing her. She pressed the button.

"Ahhh," Wanda said, clapping her hands like a three-year-old on Christmas morning.

"It works," Peter shouted.

Renee glanced at the projection. She turned fully around. What she saw was herself, wearing the gown that was in the book. *She* was the hologram. The gown glittered as if it was real.

Pressing the button again, the office went back to normal. For a long second, the three of them looked at each other. Then they rushed together and shouted in a group hug.

"You try it," Renee said to Wanda.

Wanda smiled and stood up. She walked to the place Renee had stood and pressed the button of a second prototype. It worked like magic.

"Look at me," Wanda crooned. "I love this." She twisted around, checking the dress from all angles.

"Especially the shoes," Pete chimed in.

Renee looked at the red sneakers on Wanda's feet. She usually wore high heels, but after seven this evening, she'd changed into more comfortable footwear.

"What about you, Pete? Try it," Wanda encouraged, already removing her device.

"Those are women's gowns."

"Yep, and you're a man." She made fists and raised her arms, imitating a macho bodybuilder. Pete was far from a body-builder, but he was lean and tall and the women in her office checked him out every time he passed.

"We could just as easily create a tuxedo for the men," Wanda stated.

"We should have done that," Pete said, his voice indicating he'd love to work on another project.

"One magazine at a time," Renee cautioned.

"Come on, Pete. Show us your feminine side." Wanda clamped the projection device on his arm and stood back.

With a heavy sigh Pete stepped into place and pushed the tiny pink button. The two women broke into gales of laughter.

"We'll have to redo your hair." Wanda could hardly get the words out.

Pete hit the button again, killing the image of himself. "I've seen my feminine side, and it sucks," he said.

They laughed again. A moment later, Renee heard the main entry buzzer sound.

"Expecting someone?" she asked. Blank stares looked back at her.

The three of them headed for reception.

"Carter," Renee said.

"What's he doing here?" Pete whispered. Both Wanda and Pete knew Carter owned Hampshire Publications, but they didn't know anything about her relationship with him.

"It's all right," Renee said. "I'll take care of this."

The door clicked. She pushed it open and stepped outside. It locked behind her.

"I came up to say hello, but I heard a shout. Is everything all right?"

"Everything is fine."

"It's pretty late," he said.

She looked at her watch, only there was no watch there. The device was still in place.

"What's that?"

"Just something I was working on." She put her hand down, slipping it behind her back. "You're here very late."

"I had to catch up on the work I missed when my dad was sick."

"How is your dad?"

"Almost back to his normal self." He smiled. "That means he's being a pain to everyone around him."

"What about your mom? Is she all right?"

"She asked about you."

Renee looked up at him.

"She wanted to thank you for all your help."

Renee smiled. "I didn't do much."

"And she said she'd like you to come to dinner when everyone is better."

"That would be nice," Renee said. She didn't want to commit to anything.

"Are you finished here for the night?" he asked. "I'd like to take you to get something to eat."

Renee hesitated.

"I owe you. You were there when I needed you. Be gracious enough to accept."

Renee glanced behind her.

"Don't mind us," Wanda shouted through the glass door. "Pete and I have plans."

Renee knew Pete and Wanda had no relationship that didn't involve a computer.

"It's a little late for a meal. I think I'll just go home. We have a ton of work to get done in the next few weeks."

"Then I'll see you home," Carter said.

Renee couldn't think of any reason to refuse, especially since she could see Wanda gesturing for her to accept.

"Let me get my things."

When they were on the street, Carter took her hand and threaded it through his arm. Renee felt his strength. She didn't try to pull free, but knew if she wanted to, Carter wouldn't allow it. Taking a cue from him, she leaned her head against him.

They walked several blocks, sauntered through Grand Central Terminal and got a taxi at the 42nd Street entrance. Renee gave her address and the taxi pulled into the evening traffic.

Renee settled herself against Carter in the back seat.

"Tired?" he asked.

"It was a long day," she yawned. "But a productive one."

"What were you working on so late? You haven't launched, so it couldn't be the deadline for getting everything to press."

"Just a few projects. But we'll be ready soon." *And then all will be revealed.*

The taxi stopped in front of her house and they both got out. Carter saw her to the door and said goodnight, but he didn't leave. Renee looked up at him, and he quickly pulled her to him and clamped his mouth to hers.

It was the kind of kiss that said they couldn't deny each other. They couldn't go on as they had in the past. The world for them had changed, and they must change with it. It was a new beginning kiss, an I-know-we've-been-apart-but-we're-back-now kiss. Renee raised her arms and circled his neck, giving up any thought. She wanted Carter.

The waiting taxi beeped his horn reminding them that he was there. Carter lifted his mouth and sighed into her hair. He pushed her back and looked into her eyes.

"One day I'm going to kiss you inside a place where there are no steps, no train platforms and no waiting taxi."

A free weekend. Renee couldn't think of the last time she'd had one of those. As a consultant, her weekends were booked with weddings. Since returning to New York, she'd put in weekend hours too numerous to count at *Designed for Brides*. And as soon as they launched the magazine, she'd have precious little time, so she decided to take a day off from the office.

Finally, all the boxes sitting on the floors of the various rooms in her house had been unpacked and their contents stored. Renee sat on the floor of her home office surrounded by bridal magazines. She wanted to refamiliarize herself with the competition. For the most part, the magazines were the same. There were full-page photos of bridal gowns, ads for tuxedo rentals, accessories for the bride and her bridesmaids.

Designed for Brides needed something more. Something unique that would set it apart from the many bridal magazines on bookstore shelves and newsstands. Renee leafed through the pages. While the gowns were gorgeous, nothing really spoke to her.

After going through the issues for several hours and reading everything in them, an idea struck her. But she needed help.

She needed Wanda and Pete.

Renee had an idea, but her skills were only rudimentary for executing it. Maybe Pete could do it. If not, they might have contacts. Renee liked the talkative woman and the quiet spoken man.

Picking up a magazine, she looked down at the cover. It was from Carter's company. Renee analyzed the elements. She pulled eight other magazines and spread them out in front of her. They could be mirrors of each other. All had a bride on the cover, usually the one that some designer had paid to have there.

For *Designed for Brides,* she would have control over what went on the cover. They were going to go with one of Teddy's creations for the first issue. Brides expected to see a dress on the cover — it was a mental trigger as to what was inside, what they could expect. Renee wouldn't tamper with that, but she wanted to present it differently. Taking another look at the covers, she perused them one by one, giving each one enough time to determine if there was anything that stood out to her. If she was a bride and looking for a magazine, she'd choose the one with the dress that most appealed to her. The dress on *The New Bride,* distributed by News Publications, Inc. was the one she'd choose.

She spent another twenty minutes looking at *The New Bride,* then decided she'd need more time to come up with a presentation.

Renee got up just as her doorbell rang. She turned toward the door, staring at it as if she could see through the heavy wood. She wasn't expecting anyone. She looked through the peephole and found Carter standing there. What could he want?

She opened the door. "Carter, I wasn't expecting you."

She held the door close to her arm, not opening it fully.

"Is it all right if I come in?"

Renee reluctantly opened the door and stepped back. Carter entered and she closed it.

"Would you like something to drink?

"I'll have what you're having."

She'd opened a bottle of wine, and a single glass sat on the coffee table. She got him a glass then resumed her seat.

"Buzz is all over the building that something secret is going on."

"Did you come to see what it was?" she asked.

"Just looking for ideas," he said.

Renee gathered the array of magazines and put them in a pile. "That's exactly what I was doing. I'm trying to find something that will appeal to brides and not be the same designs they've seen before."

"I believe I've heard you say that before."

"Carter, is there something you wanted? You've never been one to steal ideas, so I don't think you're here to see what I'm doing. And since we're rivals, you can't be here to help."

"I thought you might want to go out for a cup of coffee or a glass of wine." He saluted her with the wineglass.

"Well, you don't drink coffee, and we already have the wine."

"Then how about we just walk. You've been locked in here all day. A little exercise might do you good."

He couldn't know she'd been in all day, but Renee didn't argue the point.

She couldn't dispute that she needed exercise. She was a jogger, and in Princeton she'd had a daily routine of running through town before she began her day. After moving to New York, most of her energy had gone into working, first *on* the office, then *at* the office. Even her nights were filled with analyzing her competition.

"Come on." Carter offered her his hand.

Renee stared at it. Yet her heartbeat went up a notch and she found her hand moving into his. Grabbing her keys and purse from the hook by the door, she followed him out into the late afternoon.

The park wasn't that far away and they walked toward it. Carter kept hold of her hand, and Renee felt hers grow clammy.

Three years, Renee thought. She remembered the office party where they'd first gotten together. He worked on thirty-eight, and she was two floors below that, but he often came to discuss things with Blair. When the McGuinn deal had been signed, sealed and delivered, the champagne had been brought out and a celebration had begun.

Carter had congratulated her and everyone had toasted to the huge contract. When the cases in the office were all empty, they continued at a local bar, where more wine was drunk and the loud music made others get up to dance. Carter didn't ask her to dance, but she happened to bump into him. They'd laughed and talked and finally danced. As the night wore on and people began to leave for trains and buses, she found herself next to him.

His car service arrived and he offered to take her home. That had been the turning point. From the moment Renee made the decision to allow him to drive her home, her life would never be the same. She couldn't go back and change history, even if she wanted to. And she wasn't sure she did.

She'd been as happy as any of the brides displayed on the covers of their magazine. She'd thought the relationship would follow the normal cycle. But that wasn't what happened.

Renee looked at the ground and shrugged the memory off. She'd walk and not think about what was happening. Nothing was happening. Their relationship was in the past and it had no future. She was on one side of the magazine playing field and he was on the other. There was no crossing the barrier.

Renee couldn't say she hadn't thought of resuming a relationship with Carter. It had been on her mind since her heart lurched in the restaurant that night she'd met Blair for dinner.

She'd told herself they were competitors, but that wasn't the complete truth. She was just plain scared of having her heart broken again. What if the chase was all that interested Carter? What if something or someone else came along and he decided to leave without discussing it with her? Could she go through the heartache again?

That wasn't how a relationship worked. Renee hadn't been seriously involved with anyone since Carter. She'd had dates. She'd gone out with people she liked, but none of them touched her heart the way Carter had.

"Are we just going to walk or are you going to tell me why you felt the need to come to see me today?" Renee finally asked when they reached the park. Carter made her nervous, especially when he showed up without notice. His unexpected arrival at her doorstep was no different.

"I wanted to see you?"

Her heart lurched again.

"I went to your office, but all I could get out of your receptionist was that you'd taken the day off.

"I needed some down time," she said, looking away from him.

"But you spent the day working from home."

She didn't say anything, she couldn't deny it. The array of magazines he'd seen on her floor told him she had been working, but it wasn't the tiring kind of work that took all her energy when she was in the office. Maybe because she knew Carter wasn't an elevator ride away from her.

"What did you do today?" she asked.

"I thought of you."

Renee stopped as if a barrier had been placed in front of her and looked at him. Her throat went dry. She couldn't speak.

"We've got to talk about us sooner or later." Carter's stare was direct and unwavering. "Don't say there is no us. We both know that's not true."

"Carter, I can't go through that again."

"I won't ask you to."

"Don't you think it would be better if we —"

"No," he didn't let her finish. "Our emotions won't allow it. It doesn't matter how far or fast we run, we're supposed to be together."

Renee remembered them continually running into each other when she was trying to avoid him. It was like some type of force that kept putting them in the same place and time.

"And you didn't know that three years ago?" she asked.

Renee watched as Carter winced.

"I did, but it was out of my control."

"But you feel that you have control now? That nothing else will come up and force you to leave again."

He nodded. "I can't speak for the future. No one can. But I know that I will never make the same decision as I did before. I know I want you in my life. And you know it too. No matter how much you try to deny it. All I need to do is touch you and . . ."

He didn't need to finish the sentence. Renee's body reacted to his words.

"I can't do this now, Carter."

"Can't do what?"

"I can't concentrate on you and me. And I'm not saying that there is or will be a you and me. I have a lot riding on this magazine. I'm being tested with this project. Not so much by Diana and Teddy, but by myself. There's a whole industry out there and not all of them are rooting for me. I have confidence that I know what I'm doing. But I can't afford any missteps or any distractions. Can you understand that?"

"I understand," he said, although Renee wasn't sure he did. She could hear the disappointment in his voice.

"Does this mean you'll give it some thought once everything is done?"

"I will, Carter," she said. "When this magazine is put to bed, I'll think about it."

The truth was Renee hadn't been able to think of anything other than her and Carter. He'd given her some room. She didn't run into him every night or find him waiting in the reception area of her office. However today she expected to see him.

Renee was at the Magazine Expo trade show, admiring the Hampshire Publications booth. It covered the space of ten booths. The staff was mainly marketing and sales people. Renee didn't know many of them, but there were a few left over from her days.

She noticed the bridal section was bright and had a large part of the real estate, but not the greatest amount. That went to magazines on fitness and sports. Renee spent several hours walking through the show and looking at what publishers chose to display. Market share was obvious to anyone who knew how to see it.

She headed to News Publications, Inc. Their space wasn't as large as Hampshire's, but it was close, and they also had a bridal section.

"Surveying the competition?"

Renee turned to find Blair next to her.

"I am," she answered honestly. "I've already been to Hampshire. Frankly, I thought the section for brides would be larger."

"We have an adequate showing."

"It's impressive," Renee said. They did have an impressive showing, but in the back of her mind, she felt Blair was unhappy. She was smiling, but there was a sadness in it. Renee had seen that before.

"I have to get back over there. If you have a moment, have lunch with me."

"I can't. I already have plans."

Renee was seeing one of the wedding gown designers over lunch, and she would be discussing using some of his designs in her magazine. Justin Millard was relatively new to the business and she felt she had a good chance of picking him up before the world of fashion understood that he was destined to be a force in the business.

Renee said goodbye to Blair and left the expo for her appointment. She and Justin were getting together off-site — Renee didn't want any prying eyes to notice who she was meeting. Teddy had brought him to Renee's attention. Both had looked at some of his designs and felt they would augment her magazine. Justin came prepared for a presentation, even though they were in a restaurant. Renee looked through his work, forgetting her meal. She liked what she saw, and when she emerged an hour later, they had an agreement. One of Teddy's designs would be on the front cover, but Justin would get the center of the magazine. He went away smiling and agreed to come to the offices in a couple of days so they could finalize everything.

Renee went back to the convention center after lunch. The crowds were now massive, and she ended up only a row from the Hampshire display when she came face-to-face with Carter.

"Well, hello."

Renee nodded. Seeing him was like getting a narcotic elixir pumped into her blood. "I saw Blair. Things appear to be going well." She glanced toward the booth, but the crowds prevented her from seeing straight through.

Carter looked in the same direction. "I guess you'll be here next year with your own displays."

"Probably not as large as the one Hampshire is taking up, but I put in a request." The trade show was a major event for sales and marketing. Booking space a year in advance was common.

"You were always thinking about the business."

Carter smiled at her and suddenly she wasn't thinking of business at all. She had a mental picture of the two of them rolling around on the bed. Business had been the last thing on her mind then.

"It gives me something to do between breakfast and dinner." She almost said between breakfast and bedtime, but caught herself. She didn't want any references to bed.

"What do you do after dinner?"

Color rushed up her face into her hair. Renee had walked into that one. "I sometimes go out with friends."

"Anyone I know?"

"I doubt it," she teased."

Renee didn't ask if there was anyone in his past. She knew there had to be, but she didn't care to have it confirmed. It had been three years, and there could have been many women between then and now. Knowing Carter had shared his days and nights with someone else tortured her. Renee pushed aside any thoughts of Carter and another woman. She focused on the magazines in front of her, but saw only a blur of color.

"Renee." She heard her name called and turned to see a friend rushing toward her. "I've been looking for you. That guy you wanted to meet is in the booth now. Come with me."

Renee looked at Carter. "Jean, this is Carter Hampshire of Hampshire Publications," she said. "Jean Raymond. She's the —"

"Art director at Wineman and Sons," Carter finished for her.

Jean offered her hand and the two shook.

197

"Your reputation precedes you," Carter said.

"As does yours," Jean replied.

"Carter, I'll see you later," Renee said. She was glad to have a reason to leave the aura that seemed to surround him. Renee felt as if she couldn't pull air into her body whenever he was near.

"I need to get back, too. Nice meeting you, Jean." He left them.

"What a hunk," Jean said. "Who knew he was so good looking? Much better than any photo I've ever seen of him."

"Where's the booth?" Renee asked.

She glanced toward Carter's retreating back before the crowd swallowed him up.

CHAPTER 8

It had been a mistake to let her go, Carter thought making his way back to the Hampshire booth. Not only was she beautiful, but she was intelligent and had a sense for the market. He had no doubt that the magazine she was developing would be a success. He'd seen what she had done with his own bridal magazine. And she had Theresa Granville designs. They were new to the market, a fresh look, and from the reports he'd seen women were falling over themselves to get one of her originals.

That alone would make the magazine sell. But he felt Renee had another surprise up her sleeve. She was an innovator. He wasn't totally unaware of her methods as a wedding consultant. She'd done some pretty fantastic weddings. Even though he was two floors above the bridal division at Hampshire, Blair often came up to give him a rundown of Renee's work. She was good at

199

what she did.

He wouldn't do anything to discourage or sabotage her efforts, but he wished she was on his side instead of part of the competition.

He wasn't sure what would happen between them after she launched, but he was determined to make sure any conflict between them was settled.

Launch day for *Designed for Brides* was only a breath away, but before that the marketing department had set up a prelaunch party to get the buzz about the magazine started.

Every detail of the demonstration was ready, and it was time to share it with the world. Renee inhaled deeply, glancing at her staff. Wanda, Pete, and her marketing director, Stacy Costain, each gave her a smile and a double thumbs-up.

"We're ready," Stacy whispered encouragingly.

Renee walked to the head of the room. An array of bloggers, journalists, trade publication executives and influential news people stopped their conversations.

"By now you're all wondering why you were required to sign a confidentiality agreement before entering."

There was a smattering of laughter and a few groans that followed.

"The windows have been blocked, the waitstaff has left the room and there is security outside the doors."

A murmur went through the crowd.

"Don't worry," Renee stated. "We haven't locked you in. However, it's extremely important that we keep what you're about to see confidential until our magazine, *Designed for Brides,* launches." She paused. "We're giving you a sneak peek at our creation so you can have your blogs, columns and interviews ready to go in three days when the magazine hits the newsstands."

Renee surveyed the gathering. They looked inquisitive, skeptical and confused.

"You should all have received your wristband. We're called it a DR Device. DR stands for Dress Rehearsal, and it allows every bride to instantly see what she looks like in a designer gown."

Looking at the doorway, Renee saw the staff was ready. Again they gave her smiles and nods.

"Ladies," she said, extending a hand to them. Her staff funneled into the room carrying the first edition of *Designed for Brides.* It had a slick cover sporting the latest gown by Teddy. They placed copies of the magazine in prearranged locations, then moved to stand behind Renee.

"Wanda," Renee called.

Wanda walked to the center of the room amid applause. Smiling, she turned around in a full circle as if she was a runway model.

"Wanda has agreed to demonstrate. Please notice her attire *and* her shoes." Dressed in multicolored leggings with a long red T-shirt and her signature stiletto heels, she looked nothing like a bride.

"Show them," Renee said.

Pushing the pink button of her DR, Wanda's projection flashed across the open space, showing her dressed in the gown from the magazine's cover.

A collective *ahh* came from the crowd. Renee watched as eyes opened wider and mouths dropped. Three seconds of silence held the room in awe before questions flew from frenzied reporters.

"How did you do that?" someone called.

"Does mine work?" came another.

Others shouted louder, each trying to be heard and to get an answer. Questions came fast and from every direction. Renee fired replies as fast as she could.

The chaos died down and Wanda pressed her device button, returning her image to her personal attire. The room quieted and Wanda joined the small group behind Renee.

"Your devices are operational," Renee told the assembly. "Feel free to try them."

"It's working," Pete stated as the room filled with projections of one of the four gowns that beamed from the open books.

"We're going to stomp the competition," Stacy said. "I can hardly wait to see it."

"I want to see the look on Mr. Carter Hampshire's face when he hears about this," Pete said.

Renee turned to look at him.

"And when he sees it," Wanda said, then she noticed Renee's stare. "I mean, he's handsome as the devil, but he's got nothing like this."

"No," Renee agreed. "He's got nothing like this."

"What's going on down there?" Carter asked the moment Blair came into his office.

"I haven't been able to find out anything. The glass doors are blacked out and anyone who's come out of there refuses to speak about what they learned. The only thing that appears strange is they're all wearing a bracelet."

"A bracelet?" Carter's brows rose.

"The same bracelet. It has a little pink jeweled button on it. When I asked what that was for, the only thing I got was that it was a gift for attending."

Carter paced the room. Renee was up to something. It had to be big if she'd gotten the bloggers and media people to remain closed-mouthed about what was going on.

"I heard they had to sign a nondisclosure agreement. So they can't talk about what happened."

"Nothing here has ever been that secret." Carter spoke more to himself than to Blair.

"I know. There were even hired guards. I tried to get in, but my name wasn't on the list and they barred me totally. I tried every approach, even called Renee's cell. I got a message saying the line wasn't accepting calls or voice mail."

"She launches in three days," Carter said. "Someone has to know what happened."

"True," Blair said. "I know it's intriguing, but it doesn't really affect us."

Carter glared at Blair. "Our sales are declining. This is a new venture by someone who used to run our bridal division. She's planning something that directly affects us."

Blair walked to where Carter stood. Putting her hand on his arm, she turned him to face her and looked directly into his eyes. Carter didn't want her to see anything there for fear of what he might reveal, but he didn't look away.

"What's this really about?" she asked. "In three days we'll know everything. We've never been this concerned about a start-up before. Is it the magazine that's bothering you, or is it Renee?"

Carter kept his eyes from wavering. Several answers flashed through his jumbled mind, but in the end he opted for the truth.

"A little of both."

Blair waited a moment before dropping her head and her hand. "Did you answer her invitation yet?"

Carter cleared his throat. It was suddenly clogged.

"It doesn't matter," Blair said. "Like I said, we'll know everything in a couple of days."

Blair left him staring through the window. He looked down wishing he could see into Renee's offices. But more than that, he wanted to see into her mind. What was going on there? He hadn't seen her in a week. And when he left the office each night, he'd pass a delivery guy bringing in food for the whole staff on the 18th floor.

The truth was, Carter wanted to see

Renee. He wanted to be close to her, to spend time together, eat together, and make love early and often. He wanted to know if she was thinking of him. Did their conversation in the park have an affect on her? He realized it was a gradual process with Renee. Their history put an obstacle in his way and negotiating it was a delicate operation. He was making progress, but it was slow.

Renee no longer flinched at his touch or pushed him away when he got close enough to take her arm. She accepted his kisses and he knew his touch penetrated her defenses. But he wanted more, and he was sure she did, too. Even if she refused to admit it. Yet their history had burned her deeply. Somehow they needed to reach a point where she would allow herself to trust that their relationship had enough strength and promise to survive a future together.

The entire staff from Weddings by Diana arrived for launch day. The magazines hit the stands at four o'clock in the morning, and Renee hadn't been able to sleep the previous night. Her stomach was tied in knots when she stepped into the office. The day looked ordinary. They wouldn't know anything about the sales until later in the morning.

Would her plans work? As she'd hoped, buzz about the magazine had been building in the streets of the bridal district. Phone calls and email had clogged their lines and inboxes, but her staff had remained tight-lipped. The bloggers' help was greater than she'd anticipated — they were already alluding to a coming tide of change, without saying what it was. But they invited their readers to return on launch day for the anticipated reveal. Preorders of the magazine tripled as Renee had expected. And she'd been approached by the morning shows to appear because of her *revolutionary game changer,* their words. She'd agreed, and now she found herself in the studios of one of the major morning talk shows. Teddy and Diana were with her for moral support, but Wanda opted to watch from her apartment. And Pete said he wouldn't miss a single moment of the unveiling.

Renee's knees knocked as she was led from the greenroom to the on-air studio. She was microphoned and seated. Teddy gave her a smile and a thumbs-up signal as the lights came on and the anchor took her chair. Pete smiled, something he didn't do often. Renee relaxed as the interview began.

It was customary to invite your competition

to the launch party. It was also usual for them to refuse. But Carter and his bridal division staff accepted. Rumors abounded about something radical, brand new, never before seen that was coming from Renee's new venture. Unfortunately, he hadn't been able to discover what it was. He'd gone to her offices, and while she no longer barred him from her presence, she was extremely uncommunicative about what her plans at *Designed for Brides* involved.

The party would begin at eight in the evening, and it was only seven in the morning now. Carter knew she was on a talk show today; she'd mentioned it herself during one of his drop-in visits. He'd picked up one of her magazines from the newsstand in the lobby on his way to his office.

There didn't seem to be anything different except a few thick pages. Soon he and the rest of the industry would find out what all the hoopla, not to mention secrecy, was about. In the back of his mind, he closeted the hope that she'd live up to the implied promise. Anything less would devastate her and kill her business, not to mention the impact it could have on their relationship. Carter switched on the live streaming of her interview on his computer.

He'd missed her introduction and the

quick banter thanking Renee for appearing. The commentator went right to the meat of the interview.

"Ms. Hart, from what we've seen, you're about to revolutionize the magazine industry."

Renee's face filled the screen. She could be a model herself. She looked gorgeous in a high-necked lace dress that could have been a wedding gown. The unexpectedness of it hit him like hot water. He thought about the photo Dana had mistakenly sent him. Renee would be a gorgeous bride, and he wanted her to be his.

The launch of a magazine wasn't usually newsworthy. Crossing his arms, he paid silent homage to Renee for the marketing efforts she was orchestrating. Yet he was still a little apprehensive that she could pull this off.

"We have a new invention that will allow every bride to model the designer wedding gowns in our issues," she said.

Carter frowned. This was the rumor he'd heard.

"There's nothing strange about that. Brides often try on as many as twenty dresses before they find the one they wish to buy," the commentator said.

Renee smiled. Carter could tell by the way

his heartbeat accelerated that there was more to come, and she knew it.

Then he noticed the bracelet on her arm, a black velvet strap holding a rectangular box the size of an elegant watch. In the center there was a stone that looked like a pink tourmaline or pink topaz. It was faceted and shaped like a heart. Blair had mentioned this gift item when Renee held her secret meeting.

"That's the average," Renee was saying. "But many don't get to try on the designer dresses they find in magazines."

Then the commentator asked the question that was on Carter's mind.

"How is your magazine going to make that happen?"

"May I demonstrate?" she asked.

The commentator nodded. Carter moved closer to the screen.

Renee stood up and took a step forward. Whatever she faced, the camera didn't show. While she positioned herself, the commentator continued.

"This is the new magazine, *Designed for Brides.*" The anchor held the glossy cover up to the camera. Carter noticed the design, the placement of text on the cover, the font used as a branding element. It was well designed. He wouldn't expect any less of a product that had Renee's name attached to it. And it was the same magazine that lay in the center of his desk.

The camera panned back so both Renee and a portion of the studio floor were visible. Nothing appeared in front of her. Raising her arm, she pushed the pink heart on the bracelet and a life-size version of herself seemed to step off the page and become a 3-D projection on the floor in front of her. She appeared to be fully dressed in the gown shown on the cover. There was an audible gasp from the crew in the newsroom.

Carter, in his office, gasped, too.

The anchor never lost a beat or showed surprise in his voice. "As you can see, Ms. Hart has a method that will basically take your breath away. It's something every bride can do in her own home. Tell us what you've done," the anchor prompted.

Carter's phone rang. Not taking his eyes off the screen, he picked it up and pushed the accept button.

"Are you seeing this?" Blair's voice boomed through the phone.

"I'm not sure I am."

"How did she do that? Do you realize this magazine will cause a rush for the newsstands?"

"Calm down, Blair."

"We don't have anything like this. You don't even have a director for the bridal division. I've been keeping up with it. But this . . ."

She trailed off, allowing him to hear what Renee was saying. "We have a patent pending on this technology, so I can't reveal how it's done."

"Damn," he cursed to himself. They'd locked up the process.

Carter was torn. In front of him was the woman he loved, and she'd outdid him. Beaten him at a game he should know. He'd been in this business for decades. She had only taken it up a few years ago.

Carter didn't want Blair to know how he felt. Renee's creation wouldn't just change things, it would turn their world upside down. She now had a huge advantage over every other magazine on the market, and not just bridal magazines. Her innovation had the potential to change how people read, how they worked, how they shopped. Even if the magazine failed, the royalties she could charge for this technology could eliminate their competition.

Where had this idea come from? And why hadn't anyone on his staff thought of it? Why wasn't *she* on his staff? Because three years ago he'd told her they had no future.

He wondered how many other competitors were suddenly planning to attend that launch party.

The phones were already ringing on every desk when Renee walked into the office. The receptionist was trying to take messages. She thrust a handful of papers at Renee. "Your voice mail is full," she said. "And I can't answer them as fast as they're coming in."

Renee went to her office. She was still dressed and made up for the cameras.

"They're sold out," Wanda, followed by Stacy, joined Renee as she reached her desk. The smile on her face was ear to ear. "I went by three places a few minutes ago. Every magazine seller said the people descended on them in droves to get copies. One said he never saw a launch issue sell out so fast."

Renee's phone rang. She looked down at the display. It was from News Publications, Inc. Renee knew no one there, but she was sure they wanted her to answer the same questions she'd answered on the morning show.

"Do we have any more copies?" she asked.

"Sales reps have been calling for the last

hour asking for more," Stacy answered. "Marketing had the second printing released. Orders will be filled within the hour."

"Good."

The day went by that way. The phone rang every few seconds. Everyone in the office was on phone duty. By noon, things calmed down as the second delivery was being made.

"Whew," Wanda came in. "I never thought I'd hate answering a telephone, but today I could do without this invention."

Renee looked up from her desk. "You'll have time to relax. And the party is tonight."

"I hope I'll have enough energy for it."

The phone on Renee's desk rang again. She smiled and automatically picked it up.

"How's your day going?" Carter asked.

His was not the voice she expected to hear. "It's going fast," she answered, giving nothing away. She had the feeling Carter knew exactly how her day had begun and how it was at this very moment. "Why do you ask?"

"It's your launch day and I see your issue is making history. That is if television can be believed."

Ahh, Renee thought. "You saw the morning news."

"Me and several million media professionals, I'm sure."

Renee smiled. Just hearing his voice made her heart beat fast.

"Those who didn't see it are probably burning up the internet getting a look at the phenomenon. And the lucky ones who already got a copy of the magazine aren't doing any work today. They're too busy looking at themselves wearing a Theresa Granville gown."

Renee laughed.

"Don't laugh. Not only is every woman in my entire company doing nothing today, but you should be indicted for shutting down the workforce of the entire United States."

"We shipped some overseas too," she said, proudly.

"Congratulations!" Carter said, no detectable sarcasm in his voice. "You've pulled off the coup of the fashion century."

"Thank you."

"What time should I pick you up for the party tonight?"

Renee hesitated. Her heart jumped to see him, but caution was still necessary. "Carter, that's probably not a good idea. You're the competition."

"With the excitement going on over the

magazine, I doubt anyone will notice who you walk in with."

"You are wrong. I have guests from my parent company to entertain. I'll see you at the party, and I'll make my own way there."

"As you wish," he said.

Renee could hear his smile through the receiver. She also heard a whoop of laughter in the background.

"I'd better go before Hampshire Publications has to declare today a holiday for every female employee, as well as some of the men, who are ogling them in wedding gowns."

"Is one of them you?" She couldn't resist asking.

"I only ogle you," Carter said. "In case you don't know, you look beautiful in a wedding gown."

Renee was riding on adrenaline alone. She'd been rushing around all day. The only downtime she'd had was the few minutes she'd used to talk to Carter. His comments had made her face hot and her cheeks bloom with its own internal makeup. Then the frenzy had begun again with more newsstands and stores clamoring for the magazine. All copies except the ones needed for the party had been sent out.

It was going to be tight, Renee thought as she got home with barely enough time to dress before the limousine picked her up. She put the finishing touches on her outfit then stepped into the limo, which drove her to the Waldorf Astoria for the party. A separate limousine picked up Diana and Teddy, and brought them, along with their husbands, to the event. And it was an event worthy of a Hollywood premiere. The weather was beautiful, warm with just the hint of a breeze. The car pulled up to the curb, and the door opened. Renee took the driver's hand and stepped out.

Inside, Renee was one of the first to arrive. Wanda and Pete were already there. The event planners were checking all the details. Fifteen minutes later, the first guest walked in — Carter.

As hostess, Renee was at the door. He leaned down and kissed her cheek. "You look good enough to eat," he whispered. She turned her head and smiled. His mouth was very close to hers, and she wished she could kiss him. She wore a strapless gown of deep purple, and the full skirt was made of huge roses that ended in a small train. Dotted here and there throughout the roses were sparkling crystals that caught the light.

Behind Carter, Renee heard a noise. His

arrival started the parade of guests. Renee shook hands and greeted people she knew: suppliers, vendors, bridal shop owners and competitors' company executives. Some were strangers, but she knew they were there to find out what she, Wanda, Stacy and Pete had done to create the sensation that was storming the day. As soon as the morning show had aired, the phone calls had come in from people who wanted to come and had missed the date to RSVP.

They all had an excuse, but neither Renee nor the agency handling the party details was surprised. They'd planned for them at Stacy's insistence.

Dana came in at the end of the first wave. "I'm so glad to see you," Renee said as they hugged.

"I see Carter is already here."

Renee nodded but didn't say anything.

"Are you two on better terms now?" Dana asked.

"We're civil toward each other." Renee felt bad lying to her cousin. The two had always shared everything, but how she truly felt about Carter was a secret she was keeping to herself.

Dana moved around as other guests arrived. "I'll talk to you later," she whispered and headed toward Carter.

Renee followed her progression, wondering what the two of them would talk about, since she was the only subject they had in common.

Diana and Teddy arrived, taking her attention away.

"I wasn't expecting this," Teddy said, surveying the room. "This is truly overwhelming,"

"And it's affecting the office back in Princeton," Diana added.

"Did something happen?" Renee was concerned.

"We knew it would be a sensation, but we underestimated the sales it would pull into the shop," Teddy said.

Pete and Wanda came up to them smiling. When the guys left to get drinks, Teddy explained, "We hired a temp to maintain the office while we came up for the party, but it didn't work out."

"What happened?"

"She couldn't handle the orders or the number of people in the Princeton store."

"Did she leave?" Renee asked.

Teddy shook her head. "It's our fault. You'd warned us that the magazine launch would create huge demand for the gowns, but we didn't expect the number of orders to overwhelm us this much. If it hadn't been for one of our new designers cutting a vacation short and taking over the order processing, we'd be in over our heads."

"Everything is under control," Diana said. "So we can relax and enjoy the party. But tomorrow we'll head back to help with the overload."

"I'm sorry," Renee said.

"Don't be." Diana waved her concern away. "This is the best thing that could have happened to the business. Don't think about it again. Enjoy this night — it only happens once."

They smiled and accepted the wine their husbands brought. After a sip, they went off to look at the huge posters around the room of wedding gowns.

Waiters moved through the crowd with drinks and trays of food. By eight-thirty, the incoming flux of people had slowed, and Renee left the door. Carter appeared next to her with a wineglass.

"Drink this," he said. "It's sparkling water."

How had he known she was parched? The drink tasted of lemon and bathed her throat. Renee intended to rejoin Diana and Teddy and introduce them to some of the people who'd worked hard to get the magazine launched. However, the moment she looked up from her drink, she was surrounded by magazine executives.

She knew what they wanted. To find out how she'd pulled off the holograms. And those who wanted a quick five minutes alone with her also wanted to steal her away from *Designed for Brides* and have her come and work for them.

With a smile of appreciation, Renee turned them all down. But she walked away on air.

"You look like someone who's won the lottery." Carter came up beside her as she completed her conversation with the vice president of News Publications, Inc. and moved away.

"Close," she said. Renee saw another executive heading her way. When the man saw Carter, he veered off and stopped at one of the bars. Turning to Carter, she smiled, thanking him for something he was unaware he'd done. But Renee knew she couldn't allow Carter to stay with her for long. He wasn't her protector, and he'd already made the same bid for her services as the other executives were.

"How's it going?" he asked.

"As expected," she said, trying to be noncommittal in the conversation.

"They're all vying for you to join them, or

at least have a meeting on the technology."

"Exactly," Renee said. "And like I did with you, I turned them all down." She took a moment to poke him with a purple fingernail.

"I wasn't totally turned down," he said, drawing that sexy note into his voice.

Renee's thoughts went straight to the night in his apartment. Mentally shaking herself, she dispersed the images. Across the room, the event planner waved her over; it was time for introductions and her speech. Excusing herself, Renee headed for the stage.

The band played a few bars of a song, then abruptly ended it, causing the crowd to quiet down and turn to face the bandstand. Models in wedding gowns formed a line and moved onto the stage set up for them. Posters of the inaugural issue's cover descended from the ceiling as if they were lights. They'd been especially made and sealed so they wouldn't flap in the air. Twirling on pearl ropes, they were illuminated by spotlights. On the floor, the brides stepped forward and created a circle. The music began as they faced the audience with linked arms. The wedding gowns projected in front of them. As the circle revolved, each woman's image changed to a different gown.

The audience burst into applause. The brides stopped turning and returned to their places along the edge of the floor. The projections disappeared one by one and a spotlight appeared on Renee.

She gave her short speech, thanking her team and introducing them and the owners of Weddings by Diana. Then she invited everyone to enjoy themselves for the rest of the evening.

As the music began, Carter captured her before she left the floor and pulled her into his arms for a dance. Renee said nothing. She didn't resist but went easily into his embrace. She wanted to rest her head on his shoulder and allow the music to carry her away, but she was mindful of where she was and that many of the people in the room were keeping careful tabs on her. Renee didn't want to appear to favor any of the companies that were courting her.

Yet Carter's arms were strong, and she liked the way they secured her to him, the way he whirled her through the steps. They'd danced this way before. Renee remembered that office party years ago. When she'd also found herself wrapped around Carter, and she'd wanted to stay there, live there, spend an eternity there. Tonight was no different. She could easily get lost with him, especially with the music surrounding them like invisible love strands. She heard the lyrics of a love song and knew the singer was directing them to her and Carter.

Renee allowed the night to take her away. She'd pulled off a coup in the industry, and tonight was her night.

"Renee, where are you?"

Carter whispered in her ear, but she barely heard him. Her heart was hammering and heat cocooned her in a bundle of electrical nerves.

"Renee." Carter spoke her name again.

Somewhere in her mind, she realized the music had ended. She stopped and looked up at him. Whatever was in her eyes changed what was in his. Desire was raw and obvious in their gazes.

"We'd better get something to drink," Carter said.

His voice snapped her back to reality. She looked away from him, checking to see if anyone was staring at them. Only Dana seemed to find them of interest. Carter's arm, still wrapped around her waist, led her to the bar. He ordered her more sparkling water.

"If you have anything alcoholic," he said. "You'll probably forget where you are."

Renee shook herself, remembering where she was. She had to remember that all eyes were on every move she made.

Taking his own drink, a glass of wine, he walked her away from the bar and back toward a table. Wanda and Pete were on the floor, each dancing with someone Renee didn't recognize.

"Who was that?" Teddy asked coming over when Carter excused himself.

Renee checked over her shoulder, watching Carter's straight back. "That's Carter Hampshire . . . the same one who runs Hampshire Publications."

Teddy glanced over Renee's shoulder. "Good-looking man," she said.

Renee nodded.

"You two seen to know each other well."

Renee felt the color rise in her face, but Teddy knew her story. Renee had been very open after she took the job as a consultant. Over the three years she'd worked at Weddings by Diana, she'd told Teddy the entire story of her reasons for leaving Hampshire.

"Are you two getting back together?"

Renee was shaking her head before Teddy finished speaking. "We're history."

Yet she'd promised Carter she'd think about a relationship with him after the magazine launched.

It was officially public now. She'd just told Teddy they were history.

But were they?

CHAPTER 9

Renee knew exactly how Eliza Doolittle felt after her ball. It wasn't the dancing all night that had her floating — she was high on the whole event. They had done it. With Wanda, Stacy and Pete's help, the publishing industry would never be the same.

The crowds were winding down in the ballroom, and Dana found Renee near the bathroom. "We're going to have to talk," she said.

"About something important?"

Dana smiled broadly. "About all this." She looked around, encompassing the entire room, which had thinned out a lot. Renee had a collection of business cards in her beaded bag and invitations to have lunch from at least a dozen people.

"Call me tomorrow afternoon," Renee added.

Dana hugged her, draped a silk shawl over her shoulders and started for the door.

Renee, too, was ready to leave. After saying goodbye to several more people and promising to keep in touch, Renee found herself facing Carter.

"You must be tired," he said. "Sit down."

Dead on her feet, she didn't argue. Carter knew her moods. She took a seat at an empty table. The magazine lay at her place, front side up.

Pulling a chair around, Carter sat. He reached down and took her feet in his hands. Removing her sequin-encrusted heels, he lifted her legs to his knees and began methodically massaging her insteps. Renee's eyes closed at the pleasure his strong fingers evoked. She leaned back in the chair. The sensation felt so good — too good, she thought. While she wanted it to continue, she knew better. Pulling away, she placed her feet down and slipped her shoes back on, despite the fact that her feet hurt.

"It's time for me to go," she said.

"Can I drive you somewhere?"

"I have a car service," she told him.

"Cancel it. Let the guy go home to his family. I'll drive you."

She hesitated.

"It's a drive, not a commitment," Carter said.

Renee knew his views on commitment.

228

She also knew tonight wasn't a night that she should get into a dark car with him and rest her head on his shoulder. And she was too tired to talk about them as a couple.

"He's waiting," she said. "I'd better go."

Carter didn't move to stop her when she started walking. Renee refused to turn and look over her shoulder, but she knew he was watching her.

Half an hour later, the limousine pulled up in front of her house and the driver helped her out. Thanking him, she went up the few steps to her door. She unlocked it and waved the driver away. Stepping inside, she heard a car door close and looked toward the sound. Carter smiled as he crossed the street and came up the steps.

"What are you doing here?" she asked.

"I came for my good-night kiss."

Renee was stunned. Pulling her inside, he closed the door behind them. She took a step back, but he caught her around the waist, tightening his embrace. She offered no resistance as his long arms gathered her close. Renee smelled Carter's cologne — she remembered it from a past life. Three years of feelings rushed into memory at what they had once shared.

For a moment, Renee thought of pushing him back, but she wanted to be in his arms.

For just a few seconds of pleasure, she told herself, she'd remain where she was. She relaxed, allowing her body to accept all the pleasure signals she was getting. Carter's kiss was soft on her mouth. His hands crushed the purple satin as she pushed herself closer to him. Her arms snaked around his neck and she let the full force of sensation drive her up the sensual ladder to a higher rung of pleasure. Carter's hands banded her body. They were warm as they slid up her spine to rest on the bare skin of the low-cut gown.

Delirium was setting in. Renee raised a leg up Carter's and settled between his legs. She felt his erection and the heat that told her he was aroused. The thought triggered her own arousal. She knew this was the point to push back; if she went further, there would be no return. She'd told herself this was it. Either stop or be prepared to follow this to the end.

Carter lifted his mouth from hers. His eyes held desire, but he was restraining himself.

"That was some kiss," she said.

"For me, too," he returned.

"Would you like something to drink?" she asked. The heat they'd produced with only a kiss had burned the air dry.

He shook his head.

For an eternity, they stared into each other's eyes. Neither spoke, neither moved. Then, as if there was music somewhere in the background, they began to slow dance across the foyer and into the main room. Carter held her tight, but not so she couldn't escape if she wanted to get away.

She didn't.

They were alone. No one here to see them and no one expected. Renee stopped moving. She looked up, and her eyes rested on Carter's mouth. His lower lip quivered slightly. She wouldn't have noticed if she weren't a kiss away from him. Raising her hand, she touched his mouth. He kissed her fingertips gently. Fire plowed through her skin, working in circles and folds through her fingerprints and burning through to her flesh.

Moving her hand, she pushed herself up and put her mouth on his. This time the kiss wasn't soft or chaste. It was raw, wet and hungry. His mouth assaulted hers. Their heads bobbed from side to side as sensation ran through them like lightning bolts looking for a grounding wire. Renee forgot the years of separation, forgot that she and Carter had new lives and careers. All she knew was that she wanted him, and he wanted her.

Her dress crisscrossed at the back, threaded by a white ribbon that tied at her lower back. Carter found the bow and pulled. The dress loosened and fell. Renee caught it between them. Cool air rushed against her back but was quickly replaced by the heat of his hand. When he smoothed his strong hands over her bottom, Renee instinctively seized as new arrows of electrical current shocked her. She knew his hands, knew the feel of them, the size that was perfectly fitted to the exact curvature of her body.

She ran her hands over his arms and around his back. His mouth continued to work magic on hers. His head pushed her back, bending her over as the two seemed to merge into one. Renee didn't know how her dress slipped from her shoulders. Only when Carter's hands found her bare breasts and patted his thumbs over them, causing her to utter a cry of pleasure, did she realize the dress hung near her arms.

His mouth followed his hands, and she arched toward him as the erotic stroke of his tongue introduced her to a world of sensual pleasure. Slipping her arms from the dress, it fell like a pile of purple roses around her feet. Carter lifted her out and carried her toward the stairs. Renee laid her head between his shoulder and neck, and teased his ear with her tongue as he staggered like a drunk man up the stairs.

There was a soft light coming from her bedroom and Carter headed that way. Inside he took her to the bed and slowly let her slide down his body until her feet reached the floor. He looked down at her. Renee felt as if she was the most loveable person in the world. With only his eyes, he could tell her everything she needed to know.

When he kissed her again, his mouth was back to the tender, thoroughly satisfying kiss that, despite its gentleness, wrung everything from her. It forced her to want him, to use her hands and the soft movement of her hips to tell him she was ready for him. She wanted his body merged with hers, wanted to feel their joining and wanted to enjoy the pleasure of making love.

Renee pulled Carter's bow tie loose, unbuttoned his shirt and pressed her wet tongue to his slightly moist skin. Tasting the salt of his body, she felt his hands squeeze her bottom as he pulled her tighter against his erection. Holding on to her sanity, she pushed his jacket over his arms. One at a time, he slipped his arms free. The jacket fell to the floor, but Renee was oblivious to it. Her eyes were trained on the uncovered skin of his chest. For a long moment she only looked at him. His darkened skin was smooth and contoured, as if some hand had personally outlined him, not in plaster or bronze, but in flesh and bone. Renee's throat went dry.

Yet her need multiplied. She pressed herself to him, running her hands over his shoulders and arms, feeling sparkles of electricity. Hooking her arms around his neck, she kissed him. She was only a head shorter than his six-foot frame, yet she went up on her toes. She loved the taste of him.

His breathing was hot against her mouth and her heart thumped so hard, she thought it would burst through her chest. She couldn't take this torture much longer. She needed him now. Wanted him more than she'd ever wanted anyone.

She wanted to know that the beauty they had created three years ago had only been on hold, had not died away. She brought her hands to his belt and released the buckle. In seconds they were both naked. Carter lifted her and placed her gently on the bed. He stretched out next to her, kissing her so lightly it was like being caressed, yet he was driving her wild. His mouth traveled over her contours, kissing her eyes, her mouth, her shoulders. Taking his time, he moved from one area to another. Large hands massaged her back and came around to skim over nipples that stood erect at his touch.

Carter rolled over her, cupping her face and looking down at her. Her hair had come loose from its moorings, and he threaded his fingers through it as his mouth descended to take hers. Inside her hunger and need combined to a pleasure–pain paradox. Carter reached over the edge of the bed and found his pants. In seconds, he had a condom out of its package and had placed it over himself.

Renee didn't wait for him. She pulled him down on top of her and opened her legs for his entry. When it came, her eyes fluttered. The rhythm was slow to begin, but soon changed to a frenzied pace that she didn't think she could maintain. Yet the deep pleasure drove her further and further along the ride with Carter.

Guttural sounds mingled in the air. Renee was unsure if they came from her throat or Carter's. She didn't try to distinguish one from the other. He was here. With her. She'd forgotten how good they were together, how his body completed hers, how they moved in unison and gave all. She held nothing back. Whatever she felt, she let Carter have. He filled her time and again, their bodies meeting, retreating, meeting again. Each drive had her eyes closing and her body taking in the passion that only the two of them could create.

Carter rolled her over the big bed, carrying her over and under him. Renee was immersed in the pleasure he granted her. Biting her lip, she took the pleasure his body offered her. Yet neither Renee nor Carter would give in. She reached for more and more until the scream she'd pinned inside her wouldn't remain quiet. It was about to release.

She moved, rolled, reversed positions with Carter until she was over him, her body pumping his. His hands smoothed over her belly and squeezed her breasts. The action released something wild that lay dormant inside her. Like a suddenly awakened tiger, she ravished him. Hunger for him drove her to oblivion.

Somehow they rose to a higher level than ever before. For a space of a lifetime she held the pleasure. Then she collapsed onto his sweat-slick body. Renee could say nothing. Carter's arms embraced her. Large hands roved over her back and the curve of her bottom. Their breath was ragged and loud, but the air was filled with the aftermath of lovemaking.

Carter brushed her hair aside and kissed her forehead. Renee had never felt more cherished.

Sanity returned with the sunlight that streamed through the windows. Renee smelled coffee and bacon. Opening her eyes, she pushed herself up on her elbows and looked at the empty place where Carter should be sleeping. He was gone.

"A man who cooks," she said out loud as she smiled.

Dressing quickly, she rushed down the steps and burst into the kitchen.

"You're cooking," she said needlessly.

Carter wore one of her aprons and boxer shorts. Nothing else. The sight had her body going into overdrive.

"I'm starving," he said.

He turned to face her, and Renee felt all the heat of last night's bedroom gymnastics return to claim her. Carter placed breakfast on the table. The two of them ate in silence, yet their eyes spoke, their hands talked and the smiles they offered each other told a story that only they would understand.

Over coffee and juice, the English language returned to their minds. "Shouldn't you already be at work?" Renee asked.

"I called in and told them I'd be late."

"How late?" Renee smiled tantalizingly.

"How late do you want me to be?" Getting up from the table, he came to her and pulled her out of her seat. He kissed her, long and hard. Renee tasted the juice he'd drunk. Her knees went weak, and she wondered if he'd always have that effect on her.

She lay against him when he lifted his mouth. His heartbeat was steady in her ear. She liked being where he was, felt as if this was where she belonged. But they were competitors. They were going to have to discuss their relationship soon. But not now, she told herself. Now, she just wanted to stand here in her kitchen, with the morning sun streaming in, and be wrapped in Carter Hampshire's arms.

Grand Central Terminal was packed with weekend travelers. Renee searched the cavernous structure for Dana. They'd agreed to meet by the double staircase in front of the three tall arched windows facing the main concourse. The sun shone brightly through them, and Renee squinted as she searched the room.

She spotted Dana walking across the marble floor, holding two cups of coffee.

"Do you have time?" Renee asked, accepting one of the cups.

"My train leaves in forty minutes."

They climbed the stairs and found a seat away from the moving mass of people.

"What did you think of the party?" Renee asked.

"It was wonderful!" Dana's eyes opened wide. "You and whoever created those graphics are geniuses. I imagine sales are through the stratosphere."

"They're greater than projected. And, by the way, who did you leave with? I couldn't see his face."

Dana looked down, a shy smile on her face. "He is an advertising director at Juvenock Magazines. He saw me to my hotel, chastely kissed me on the cheek and promised to call." She took a drink from her cup. "This morning, when I checked out, there was a card waiting saying he enjoyed last night and would call later today."

Renee smiled. "Maybe I should go back to being a wedding consultant for one more wedding."

Dana sat up straight. "Not so fast. We live in different states. You know that rarely works out in the long run." She smiled brightly again. "But for the time being, it might be fun."

Renee knew Dana's situation and how cautious she was with men. The loss of her fiancé had changed her. It had taken her a long time to get over that, and even longer to begin dating again. Renee was glad to think that her cousin was healing.

"What about you? Are you and Carter . . . *friendlier?*"

A frisson of emotion ran through Renee. Just hearing Carter's name raised her temperature and pumped her heartbeat.

"We're friendlier," she admitted.

"Did he ever explain why he left three years ago?"

Renee understood that was a question that Dana broached with caution. Renee took a sip of her coffee and looked Dana in the eye. She explained what Carter had told her.

"He was in Afghanistan?"

Renee nodded. "Our relationship hadn't developed very far and he didn't want to have someone worrying about him at home."

Dana sat quietly for a very long time. Renee wondered what she was thinking. Did this remind her of her lost fiancé?

"I know you might think that doesn't

sound like a good reason, but it was."

"How can you say that?" Renee asked.

"Renee, he was protecting you."

"How do you figure that?"

"Answer a question. Were you in love with him when he left?"

Renee waited a moment, then nodded.

"Did he know that?'

"Not in words. I'd never said it."

"But we all know when a relationship crosses the line and changes, matures, turns more serious."

Renee couldn't deny that. She nodded quickly even though Dana had not asked a question.

"He was saving you from pain in case something happened to him."

Renee weighed her words.

"But why didn't he tell me?"

"Because it wouldn't have spared you. If you'd known, you'd have waited, written, called. You'd have done all the things I did." She stopped.

Both women stared at each other.

"Then when you couldn't reach him by phone or mail, when you got no responses to anything, you'd have fallen off the deep end, like I did."

Renee gripped her cup with both hands. "I fell off of it anyway."

"You did, but there's a difference."

"What's that?" Renee asked.

"You have another chance. He's back, safe . . ." Dana didn't go on. Her voice cracked.

Renee reached over and squeezed her hand.

It was time for Dana's train, and the two walked to the platform together and hugged goodbye.

"Renee, think about giving him another chance."

"I'll think about it," she said. "Carter asked me to think about it too."

Dana smiled, hugged her again and got on the train. She waved from one of the windows, but her words hung in the air as the huge silver cars rolled out of the station.

The office was less frantic then it had been the day before. Renee and Carter hadn't arrived together. He'd had to go to his apartment and change clothes, and she'd had to meet Dana, but not before they had spent a long time in her shower and then again in bed before parting. Renee could still feel the evidence of their night together. Throughout the morning, she kept smiling as she remembered the two of them making love and holding each other. She wished it had never ended.

Dana's words rang in her ears. *Give him another chance.* What was last night, if not a chance?

The phones were ringing, and the office was full of flowers, bottles of champagne, some of the world's best chocolate and notes of thanks from several of the past evening's guests. Renee continued to get job offers and questions about sharing their technology from some of the publishing professionals.

News reporters wanted interviews, but Renee wanted to escape. For a short moment, she considered going up to the 38th floor and hiding out in Carter's office. But Carter was one of them — the competition that was desperate for her technology. He didn't feel like one of them when she remembered his hands on her body, but her brain knew going upstairs would be a monumental mistake.

Diana and Teddy's arrival was a godsend. Her secretary would hold all her calls, giving her some needed downtime. Now that the first issue was history, they had work to do to get the second one to press and get a head start on the next six. She'd finally feel comfortable when they were months ahead of the curve.

"Did you enjoy yourself last night?" Renee asked the two partners.

"I had more fun that I thought possible," Teddy said. "I loved the show. Those covers coming from the ceiling and the gowns in the circle . . . wonderful idea."

"You can thank Wanda and Stacy for that," Renee said. "We had an event planner, but Stacy came up with the idea."

"Which one is Stacy?"

Renee glanced through the door. Stacy was standing near her secretary. "She's the blonde right there." Both women followed Renee's nod. "She's the one who worked with me on numbers for the expected orders of gowns. We sent you the projections."

"And she was so right," Teddy commented. "From what I heard, the phone orders continue to be brisk. And we had to expand the bandwidth on our website to keep up with the traffic."

"Other than that, tell us about the man you spent a lot of time with last night," Diana asked.

"Man?" Renee asked. "What man?" Her body grew warm. She knew exactly what man they were talking about.

"The man who danced with you several times. The one who couldn't keep his eyes off you even when you weren't dancing."

"His name is Carter Hampshire. And he's the competition," Renee said. She glanced at Teddy who already knew who Carter was. Obviously, Teddy had not shared the information with Diana. Renee thanked her silently for keeping her confidence. "He owns this building, or his family does."

"And he couldn't keep his eyes off you," Teddy teased.

"I'm sure you're wrong."

"I wonder," Teddy said.

Renee left it at that. But Dana's words echoed back. *Give him another chance.*

Life fell into routine after a couple of weeks. Renee was busy working on the next several issues. Advertisers were knocking down the door, even though their prices were through the roof and they had a waiting list. Bridal designers vied for callbacks so they could secure a spot in an upcoming issue. Every one of them wanted their dress to be featured as one of the four spots that used the hologram. She referred their calls to the sales reps, but found she was constantly required to sign off on some deal.

After each exhausting day, she and Carter would continue their lovemaking at either her house or his apartment. So far neither of them had broached the subject of their relationship and the fact that they were competitors. Renee knew it would have to come sooner or later, but she'd rather it be later. Her feelings for Carter were securely in place, and she didn't want to give up her secret meetings with him.

Was it the fact that their relationship was a secret that made lovemaking so exciting? Renee didn't know and didn't care. All she knew was that she was in love with Carter Hampshire and together they created fireworks. She now understood the yearning of brides for their partners, the love that wove its way around and inside them, creating that invisible bond that seared them together. She knew the obsessive need to give, to please, to crave understanding.

Now, Renee stretched in Carter's big bed. Her hand touched his arm and he immediately took it, pulling it to his mouth and kissing her fingers. The familiar reaction to his touch sparked through her. She smiled, loving the way he made her feel. She looked up as his hand brushed her hair back, and he rolled toward her and kissed her hairline.

Renee couldn't remember ever being this happy. Her heart virtually sang every night when she knew she'd meet him. They'd cook together, have dinner, discuss everything from world politics to the price of an internet connection. Never did they talk about the magazine business. Then they'd retire to his bedroom or hers and make love throughout the night.

"What are you thinking about?" Carter asked.

"Marbles," she said.

"Marbles?" Carter laughed. Renee felt his body shake against her. "What about marbles?"

"I don't know. I don't seem to have any."

"Where did you lose them?"

They both laughed at the old joke. Renee knew where she'd lost hers. Well, they weren't lost — she'd given them away. Given them to the man holding her. Yet she hadn't told him. Not yet. But she would.

Reaching up, she kissed him, brought her lips to his and tasted the essence of Carter. His hand slipped over her bare belly and around her body. When he pulled her into alignment with him, she felt the entire length of his long, strong body. Their legs entwined and they looked into each other's eyes. It was that look that started the burning. Carter's gaze marked her as surely as if he'd touched her, and Renee felt the heat rising.

Carter fell back against the bedding. Her

body fit into his as his erection hardened and pressed into her. Renee initiated a kiss. She felt the restrained lion in him that controlled strength he held tightly until she was ready, until it was impossible not to release the tension within them.

Climbing on top of him, she stretched down his body. Moving slowly against him, she felt the ecstasy of love beginning. Carter's hands thrust into her hair and clamped over the back of her head. He held her that way for an eternity, his mouth taking hers and working its magic, the tension within her coiling and tightening. Finally, pushing her aside, he found a condom and she took it from him. Watching Carter's joy, she slipped it over him. His eyes rolled back as pleasure took control of his features and Renee slipped her hands up and down over him. His hands grabbed hers and he stopped her with a groan.

He pulled her down, reversing positions. He gazed into her eyes until she felt something snap within him. In seconds he was inside her. Passion flooded them. Fire flared into a roar and the rhythm between them moved with a fury strong enough to topple the Earth.

Renee heard herself moan at the pleasure that coursed through her. Her arms hugged him and her body matched the speed of his. Her throat was parched as she breathed through her mouth. She kissed his shoulders, his chest, as her body writhed beneath his. She grasped his shoulders, holding on as Carter pushed her legs up and took them higher on the ecstasy scale. As control was lost between them, she felt a hard wave rising. It was higher than any that had come before. Clamping her mouth closed, she waited, held back, tried to stop it from cresting too quickly.

It was impossible. The wave broke through. She felt more than heard her scream, and Carter's groan was audible in her ears. Together they climaxed and collapsed onto the bed. Renee let her breath out. Carter, lying on her, his chest taking long drags of air, as if it was a liquid he could drink.

"Wow," was all Renee could say. Even the other times they'd made love hadn't compared with this. He slid sideways and caressed her against him. Carter kissed her neck, holding her and taking long breaths. Renee didn't think he could speak — she knew she couldn't.

The way Carter made her feel was life-changing. She knew it was for him, too. Could it always be this way? Would she be able to keep this bright star of love alive in the future? She didn't know if she could, but she was sure going to try.

Something woke Renee. Turning to reach for Carter, her hand felt the coolness of the sheets where he should be lying. Her eyes flew open. Where was Carter? Glancing at the clock, she saw it was just after four o'clock in the morning, too early for breakfast. She didn't smell the coffee or the bacon that he loved to eat in the morning. Where was he?

Slipping out of bed, she grabbed one of his shirts and pulled it over her naked body. There were no other lights on in the hall. Quietly she went toward the living room. No light filtered in from the outside, but there was a light coming from his office.

Was he working?

She smiled. The man was diligent. Renee went toward the light and pushed the door open. Carter swung around in his chair. Renee looked over his shoulder, immediately recognizing her own work. *Her* layout. Her designs for upcoming issues of *Designed for Brides*.

"What is this?" she asked, her eyes fixed on the screen.

"Renee, it's not what you think."

"Those are my designs, and you have them. You stole them," she accused. "That's why you've been so good to me. You wanted them all along."

"Renee, let me explain."

"What could you say?" she shouted. "That you've been trying to get my designs? First you ask me to take a job with you. When that fails, you decide to steal what you can."

"That's not how it was."

Renee stormed back to the bedroom. Putting her clothes on over the shirt, she gathered what things were readily within reach and bolted for the door.

"Renee, we have to talk."

"We've done all the talking we need to. Get out of my sight. I never want to see you again."

Renee rushed through the door and grabbed the first taxi that came by. She held on to her tears until the driver dropped her off at her home. Inside she backed up against the door, but her knees were too weak to keep her upright. She slid to the floor and let the sobs burst.

CHAPTER 10

Blair Massey sauntered into Carter's office and slipped into a chair. "What's up?" she asked.

Carter stood behind his desk. He'd paced the entire room waiting for her to arrive. He couldn't believe what he'd seen. There had to be a logical explanation, something reasonable, something understandable.

"Have you checked our sales and projections in your division?"

She nodded. "Since Renee's launch we've been seriously down in sales, but I expect them to pick up once the wedding season is in full swing."

"This layout you sent me yesterday," Carter said, restraining his voice to something approachable. "It's wonderful, better than anything I've seen in years."

"Thank you. We strive for the best." Blair recited the bridal division motto.

"Who in the department thought of this?

I want to be sure to give credit where credit is due."

"That's just like you, wanting to give praise. The entire department worked on it, but the initial idea came from me. I'll pass your thanks on to the rest of the group."

Carter rounded his desk and sat down. He looked into the smiling face of a woman he never thought he'd have to say these words to. Blair stared back at him. After a while, she realized the serious expression on his face meant something.

"What's wrong, Carter?"

"I've seen this design someplace else."

Blair sat up in the chair. "Someone's stolen our idea?"

He didn't move, didn't nod or shake his head. "No one stole our design."

"Where did you see it?"

"On Renee Hart's desk at *Designed for Brides.*"

"How did you happen to see that?" Blair was uncomfortable. Carter knew her well and he knew how she sat, what her mannerisms were when she was nervous. She pursed her lips and licked at her lipstick.

"Why did you steal it, Blair? We don't need to do that."

She got up and stood behind the chair she'd been sitting in. "Why do you think I stole it?"

"You just admitted it was your idea."

"I did but . . . when we were working, the design just grew. No one stole it. We came up with it independently."

"Blair." Carter's voice held a warning. "You stole the design."

"Well, what did you think I would do? We needed something big to compete with her magazine. I tried to get something. The department worked night and day trying to come up with something that would make the industry look at us. Nothing compared. Then I saw the designs in her office when we had a lunch date. She got called away for several minutes. I had a jump drive with me. I always carry one — it's a habit. I can't tell you what came over me, but I put the drive in and copied it."

Carter stared at Blair as if he'd never seen her before. She'd been employed by Hampshire for over twenty years. He'd trusted her.

"Blair, you're fired."

The words stunned her. Her face paled to the point that Carter thought she'd pass out from lack of blood flow.

"Fired?"

"I have no choice. Do you know the number of laws you've broken? Do you realize your actions could ruin not only the bridal magazine division, but the entire business?"

"No one knows. Our magazine will get to the stands before hers. It'll look like they stole ours. It'll put them out of business."

"Blair, how can you even think that's something this company would have any part of?"

"It's done all the time. This is business."

"That is not the kind of business I run. And until a few days ago, not the kind you did either."

She looked at the floor, then up at him.

"You have to go, Blair."

There was nothing else to say. Blair opened her mouth to speak, then closed it. She'd done the unforgivable. And Carter was going to have to do some serious damage control, both for the company and for his relationship with Renee.

Carter lifted the phone and called security.

"Security will be here in a few minutes to escort you from the building."

Word of Blair's firing raced through the office like a forest fire. It reached Renee just before lunch. Blair had worked at Hampshire Publications for more years than some of the people there had been on the planet.

And now she was gone. Renee wondered why, but she couldn't call Carter and ask. She wanted nothing to do with him.

Was he blaming Blair for stealing her design? Was he using her as the scapegoat for his theft?

Renee's phone rang.

"Hello," she said.

"Ms. Blair Massey is here to see you."

Renee swallowed. Blair? Here?

"Shall I send her back?"

"Of course," Renee said.

What could Blair want? Maybe she was here to ask for a job. Renee stood and waited to see her come around the corner. She'd aged years in just a few hours.

"Blair," she called. "Come on in."

Renee closed the door and offered Blair a seat. She sat in front of the desk. Renee took the second guest chair next to her.

"You've heard," Blair began.

"I think by now the news has reached the Jersey Shore." Renee tried to lighten the mood that had descended on the room. She hadn't expected to see Blair. In fact, by now she would have expected Blair to be halfway home. "I'm surprised you're still in the building."

"I'm sure you are," Blair said. "That gauntlet I just passed through looked like they had their claws out." She glanced at the door.

"They're curious, that's all."

Renee looked through the glass wall. The entire office was pretending to work, but they were really trying to discover what was going on.

"How can I help you?" Renee asked.

"I believe I'm here to help you."

Renee stared straight at her, but kept her face unemotional. The comment was a lead-in to a job interview.

"All right, how can you help me?"

Blair smiled as if she knew something Renee didn't. "You're all wondering why Carter fired me?"

Renee leaned forward in her chair and stared directly at the woman. "Yes, we are. You're a staple at Hampshire Publications. You're at the top of your field, and you've run more of those magazines than anyone else. I don't understand Carter."

"It wasn't Carter," Blair said.

Renee frowned. "What wasn't Carter?"

"Carter fired me, but you're the reason I got fired."

"Me!" Renee was stunned. "How could I have anything to do with it?"

Blair hunched and dropped her shoulders. "You're good. You're brilliant. Your marketing plans are beyond great. And they sell. That thing you did with the launch magazine was historic. And not just for magazines. I've heard the reports of how other industries want to adapt it to their particular products. I could never come up with anything even remotely resembling it."

Renee felt as if she should say thank you, but it also seemed inappropriate. So she said nothing.

"Let me get to the point. You know I'm a good person. But . . ." Blair paused. "Everyone, good or bad, has a breaking point. Carter fired me because I stole them."

"You stole . . . you . . . not Carter," Renee stammered. "What plans?" Renee's heart began to beat faster.

"The ones for the next year, I copied them and used them as my own."

Renee again leaned forward. Her hands went to the computer keys on her desk.

"Don't bother," Blair stopped her. "They're there, exactly as you expect them to be. I used a jump drive to copy them the day we went out for lunch."

"How . . . I . . ." Renee stopped. She was at a loss for words.

Blair stood up as if the interview was over and she was ready to go.

"About the plans . . ." Renee began.

"Don't worry. I never got to use any of them. Apparently, Carter found out where I got the ideas. I have no idea how he knew."

Renee felt heat paint her skin.

Blair went to the door. With her hand on the knob, she turned back. Renee had the feeling she was a character in a play on Broadway. She was an understudy who didn't know her lines.

"I may not know how he got them, but I'm sure you have some idea." With that, Blair opened the door.

"Blair, one more thing," Renee said.

The woman she'd called her friend for nearly a decade turned back, her brows raised.

"Why are you telling me this? Why admit it?"

"I'm sure in the long run Carter would tell you anyway, but I admire you. I don't know what slant someone else would put on the story, but I wanted you to hear the truth. From me."

"Thank you for that."

Renee felt numb. She hadn't expected the day to go this way. She'd lost a friend and a lover. How could she have been so wrong? He'd told her he'd never do anything to encroach on her business. Yet she hadn't even given him the benefit of the doubt.

She'd immediately assumed he was there to steal. That he'd been using her all this time, just to get her designs.

But it wasn't just the designs. She hadn't trusted him. Or even given him the opportunity to explain. She couldn't blame him if he never spoke to her again.

Renee flopped against the back of her chair. She took in a long breath, feeling as if she hadn't had air since Blair had walked into her office.

Closing her eyes, Carter came to mind. She'd accused him of theft. He was innocent . . . but he must have recognized the plans. Why hadn't he told her? Maybe he thought she stole them from Blair, and not the other way around? But how had he found out the truth?

And what was she going to do now that she'd destroyed his trust?

The 38th floor felt very far away. Renee's elevator trip up to the offices of Hampshire Publications was like ascending to a high office to be called on the carpet. Carter may well throw her out, and he'd have every right to do so. She'd broken his trust. She didn't know if that could be mended. She hoped so.

The elevator doors opened onto a highly

polished hallway.

"Ms. Hart," the receptionist stood up and came around her desk. "It's so good to see you." She hugged Renee.

"I'm here to see Carter," she explained. "If you don't mind, I know the way."

For a moment the receptionist looked confused, then she smiled and pressed a button to let her through security. Renee held her head high as she walked through the door and passed several offices. Some of the people she knew gawked at her. Renee nodded to them, but didn't slow her pace. She was on a mission. Silence followed her movements. People thought she was there for a fight and that an explosion was imminent.

She saw Carter's secretary. "Is he in?" she asked, passing the woman without altering her stride.

The secretary stood up, but had no time to say anything before Renee opened the door and went inside. She closed it, hearing a click of finality. Carter turned around in his chair. The expression on his face told her she was the last person he expected to see. Her heart thundered. He could order her out. She expected him to do so.

"We need to talk," she said. "No, I need to talk."

Carter stood, but said nothing. Moving across the room Renee stood in front of his desk. She didn't sit. What she had to say needed to be said standing up.

"I apologize," she began. "Blair came to see me."

He frowned. "She did?"

"She told me the truth about the designs. That *she'd* stolen them. You didn't. It was all her."

Renee waited for Carter to give her an indication that she should go on, that there was some kind of forgiveness. She found none.

"I'm sure you don't want to see me again, but I wanted to tell you how sorry I am for mistrusting you."

"Apology accepted," Carter said.

Renee waited a moment. Neither of them seemed to have anything more to say. Renee glanced at him, expecting it would be the last time she saw him alone. She turned to leave.

"Renee." She stopped at the sound of his voice.

"You said we needed to talk. I have something to say."

She turned around.

"Please sit down."

Renee took a seat. If he wanted to level

accusations at her, she deserved them.

"I'm sorry Blair did what she did," he said. "But it forced me to make a decision. I'm going to need your help to accomplish it."

Renee frowned, then blinked several times. She had no idea what Carter was getting at. "It's about the magazines, both yours and mine."

Renee nodded, but was still confused.

"I think they should merge or —"

She jumped up as if propelled. A business deal. He was offering her a business deal? "You're suggesting I merge *Designed for Brides* with *Hampshire Bridal*?"

Carter raised his hands, palms out. "That's not what I mean."

She put her hands on her hips and stared at him. "Then what do you mean?"

"I lied to you about the bridal division at Hampshire," he said.

"How?"

"It's not doing as well as I told you it was. But that magazine is your baby. You love it and the love you feel for it is evident in the product you produce yourself. Since you left three years ago, things haven't been the same."

"And your solution is . . . ?"

"I sell Hampshire's bridal division — to you."

The silence was deafening. "Are you kidding?"

"Not in the least." Carter's face was serious.

"I sell the bridal division to you. You can either merge it with *Designed for Brides* or add it as a second magazine. The choice is yours."

"I don't understand. You're giving up the business?"

"There is one condition. Well, two conditions."

She knew there had to be a catch.

"You keep the staff. Their benefits remain intact. They're good people, and they'll put out an excellent magazine."

"I don't understand." Renee's head was spinning. They hadn't had a competitive fight, and they must still be profitable enough to make the business valuable to the larger company.

"I'll be honest with you. The magazine hasn't been pulling its weight for several years. It's reached its cycle with us. You can bring it back to life, give it another name, another look, make it successful."

"Carter, you have more experience than I do with magazines. You know how to reinvent a magazine."

"That takes a lot of work, and we don't have the manpower or creativity to do it. I have confidence that you can turn it around in a short period of time. It's why I wanted you to return to Hampshire. Since that is not possible, the decision was to close the division or sell."

He walked around the desk and came to stand in front of her. "Do we have a deal?"

"I can't make a deal like this without first discussing it with my partners."

"I understand. Then do we have a tentative understanding of a deal at least?"

"You said there were two conditions. What's the second?"

"My mother gets one of her designs featured at least once a year for the next three years."

Renee smiled, then laughed. "I think that can be arranged if we go through with this. But I'll have to see the books, and I'll need everything disclosed."

"Absolutely, I'm sure your accountants and mine will be able to work together."

"In that case, we have an understanding."

Carter thrust out his hand. Renee stared at it. She couldn't remember them ever shaking hands. And at this moment, she was afraid to put her palm against his. Slowly, she raised her hand and he took it, encasing it in his. Then he released it and returned to his desk.

"I'll have our lawyers draw up some proposals to get the ball rolling."

Renee nodded and turned to leave. She stiffened her back and walked to the door. He'd brushed her apology away as if it had meant nothing. The business deal had been more important than her telling him she was sorry.

The weight of the world got heavier and heavier as she stepped into the elevator and held on as it descended thirty-eight floors. The sun was bright as Renee walked out into the warm afternoon. She took a deep breath and dropped her shoulders.

She'd survived losing Carter once before. She could do it again. But this time she wouldn't be leaving New York or changing her profession — there was no running away. She was in love with him, but she'd killed that love with her mistrust.

Renee walked away from the building. She'd walk a while, then head for home. A long plaza led to the street. As she reached the three steps that led down to the public sidewalk, she stopped.

This was not the way it was going to end, Renee thought. Not this time. Quickly she whipped around and crashed into Carter.

"You don't think I'm letting you get away a second time, do you?" Carter asked.

"Are you . . . what are you saying?"

"I'm in love with you. I've been in love with you since you first came to work here. I couldn't risk telling you three years ago, but I love you, and I'm not letting business get in the way of our happiness."

"Carter . . ." Renee said, but had no idea what she wanted to say. "What just happened in your office?"

"I offered you a business deal and you accepted it — tentatively."

"And now you're telling me you love me," she stated.

He nodded. "I first had to clear away any obstacle between us. And the magazine was one of them. I want your love more than I want that business. Is that okay?"

"I'm sure I can handle that."

He smiled. "Is that all you can handle?" He raised his eyebrows. "Can you handle me being in love with you?"

"How do I know you won't decide to leave me again the way you did three years ago?"

"I explained where I went —"

Renee put her hand up to his mouth, silencing him. "I know," she said. "I know you can't promise that."

"But I will," he stated. "If you'll forgive me, I'll never leave you again."

"I forgave you long ago, Carter."

"But you never said anything."

"I did, just not in words. I know your decision was to protect me in case something happened to you. It was a noble gesture."

"But I understand now how unfair it was," Carter said. "I should have told you the whole truth. But I knew there was no guarantee that I'd return. If anything happened to me, I wanted you to be free."

"I would have chosen you. Even though we'd only been together for a short time, I was certain of my love. And, yes," she said, "knowing you love me means I can handle anything. Can you handle it, too? The fact that I'm in love with you?" The words came easily to her lips. "I love you," she repeated.

Carter pulled her into his arms and standing on Madison Avenue, oblivious to the crowds passing by, he kissed her. Kissed her hard and long. Kissed her with all the passion of a man in love.

Renee returned it. She had nothing to hold back. Her arms climbed around his neck and she let her heart open up. Love poured out in torrents. And she was happier than she'd ever been.

EPILOGUE

June — Twelve Months Later

The gown was a Theresa Granville. And it was real. Not a hologram. Not a projection. Not controlled by a bejeweled arm band. Renee stared at herself in the triple mirror. Dana stood behind her, a hand to her heart, her mouth open in a silent "O". Her eyes were misty, quickly filling with tears.

"Don't start crying," Renee admonished her voice full of emotion. She knew if Dana cried, her own tears wouldn't be far behind.

Dana grabbed a tissue from the box on a table in the church basement and dabbed at her eyes, careful not to damage her makeup.

"I'm not crying," she said, her voice breaking. "It's just that you look . . . you look . . ." Her hands flailed.

"You've seen me in a wedding gown before," Renee told her, remembering their dress up session.

"It wasn't real then. This time you're getting married." Again her voice broke on the last word.

Renee turned to her cousin and hugged her. After a moment, Dana pushed back, sobering.

"It's about time we started this show," Dana said, sniffing and covering her feelings.

Dana's words brought a storm of activity. The door opened and a parade of people came through it. Her mother led the group with Carter's mother right behind. Both stopped. Their hands then came up to their breasts and their mouths opened in awe. A fresh wave of emotions raced through Renee.

"You're beautiful," her mother said, her voice no louder than a prayer.

Renee swallowed, unable to reply.

Moments later the room was in utter chaos. Renee knew this was normal for the bridal party just before the ceremony would begin. The bridesmaids were all making last-minute preparations for their walk down the aisle. The chatter raised the noise level to a volume so high she wanted to cover her ears.

She'd witnessed and participated in a score of weddings. But some how everything seemed different, more pronounced, yet surreal. She couldn't explain the sensations that flooded through her, one after the other, as she stared in the mirror at herself.

She reached out at nothing in particular, but her mother grasped her hand and held it. She understood, Renee thought. Without words, her mother had come to her rescue.

Turning she hugged her mom.

"He loves you," she whispered.

"I love him, too," Renee said through the lump in her throat and the love that swelled in her heart.

"I know." Tears glistened in her mother's eyes. She blinked them away. "I could tell the first time I saw you two look at each other."

Teddy came in then. She had insisted on being the wedding consultant for *one of their own* as she'd put it.

"Time to begin," she called over the crowd. The room immediately went dead silent. With quiet authority, Teddy lined the bridesmaids up and sent them to their assigned places.

While Renee and Weddings by Diana's bridal consultants had been called upon to create some very elaborate weddings, Renee's was going to be small and simple — well, almost simple. The entire nuptials had been planned around the number two.

Both mothers stood at the sanctuary

entrance. Her mom gave her a final smile and turned to the doors. The music began and the promenade started with the two women being escorted to their seats. Renee swallowed as she waited out of sight of the guests. Her two sisters were her bridesmaids. Dana and Diana served as maids of honor.

When they were all inside and the doors had been closed, Renee imagined the groomsmen rolling out the carpet. She knew her two flower girls were excitedly peppering it with rose petals before joining the group that included two ring bearers, at the front of the church.

Teddy called Renee forward. Both her father and brother were giving her away. With an arm through each man's elbow, and her bouquet held with both hands, the wedding march began. She could hear the assembly stand. The doors opened and Renee heard an audible gasp from the congregation.

However, the only man she saw was Carter. He waited for her, appearing unnerved with a smile. It was an *only you* smile and as Renee took the first step toward her new life, she knew she'd remember that smile into her old age.

ABOUT THE AUTHOR

Shirley Hailstock began her writing life as a lover of reading. She likes nothing better than to find a quiet corner where she can get lost in a book, explore new worlds and visit places she never expected to see. As an author, she can not only visit those places, but she can be the heroine of her own stories. The author of forty novels and novellas, Shirley has received numerous awards, including a National Readers' Choice Award, a Romance Writers of America Emma Merritt Award and an *RT Book Reviews* Career Achievement Award. Shirley's books have appeared on several bestseller lists, including the *Glamour* and *Essence Magazine* lists and the Library Journal bestseller list. She is a past president of Romance Writers of America.

The employees of Thorndike Press hope you have enjoyed this Large Print book. All our Thorndike, Wheeler, and Kennebec Large Print titles are designed for easy reading, and all our books are made to last. Other Thorndike Press Large Print books are available at your library, through selected bookstores, or directly from us.

For information about titles, please call:
  (800) 223-1244

or visit our website at:
  gale.com/thorndike

To share your comments, please write:
  Publisher
  Thorndike Press
  10 Water St., Suite 310
  Waterville, ME 04901